THE SHRAPNEL ACADEMY

By the same author

THE FAT WOMAN'S JOKE
DOWN AMONG THE WOMEN
FEMALE FRIENDS
REMEMBER ME
LITTLE SISTERS
PRAXIS
PUFFBALL
WATCHING ME, WATCHING YOU (short stories)
THE LIFE AND LOVES OF A SHE-DEVIL
THE PRESIDENT'S CHILD
POLARIS AND OTHER STORIES

Plays for the stage

MIXED DOUBLES
ACTION REPLAY
I LOVE MY LOVE
WOODWORM

THE
SHRAPNEL
ACADEMY

Fay Weldon

Hodder & Stoughton

LONDON SYDNEY AUCKLAND TORONTO

The extract on page 167 is reproduced with the kind permission of the University of Chicago Press who published *The Iliad of Homer*, translated with an introduction by Richmond Lattimore, in Phoenix Books in 1961.

British Library Cataloguing in Publication Data

Weldon, Fay
The Shrapnel Academy.
I. Title
823'.914[F]   PR6073.E374

ISBN 0 340 28589 3

Henry Shrapnel, or Shrapnell, that great military genius, thought up his idea for a spherical case shot in approximately 1793. It was approved for use by the Board of Ordnance in 1803, and first used in Surinam (Dutch Guiana) in 1804. The common bursting shell had, of course, been in use since the middle of the seventeenth century; but in the same fictional spirit as we say Columbus 'discovered' America in 1492, we can say that Henry Shrapnel 'invented' the exploding cannonball in 1804.

The Shrapnel Academy is an institution dedicated to the memory of that great military genius, Henry Shrapnel – he who in 1804 invented the exploding cannonball. Bella Morthampton spent a weekend at this interesting and curious place last January. She went in the company of her lover, General Leo Makeshift, who was to give the annual Wellington Lecture; his subject was to be 'Decisive Battles of World War II'. Bella and he travelled down to the Academy on the Friday evening. Their car was a chauffeur-driven black Rolls-Royce, so plumply upholstered within it might have been a padded cell. For much of the journey the General's hand was upon Bella's knee. The interior fitments of the limousine were embossed wherever possible with the emblems of the Ministry of Defence; its windows were darkened and bullet-proof. It was surprisingly quiet inside, as is a church in a noisy city centre. Those outside, of course, could not see those inside at all; who it was who travelled in so grand and mysterious a way, though who could doubt that whoever it was had the future nicely at their fingertips. And as for the view from within, well, that was distorted by the thickness of the toughened glass panes, so that the world passed by, as intended, as if it had almost nothing at all to do with Bella or the General; neither the noble broadwalks of the central city, not the humbler, messy suburbs, nor the stark and unleaved country lanes the limousine presently manoeuvred – the Shrapnel Academy was situated in the rural heart of the country – but of course it had: it had very much to do with them, and they with it.

Bang! Bang! as the children say to each other. Bang, you're dead!

Bella posed as the General's secretary, at his request. He wished to live comfortably with his wife – an innocent and elderly soul – and avoid scandal, and why should he not? Bella wore a tight black skirt and seamed tights and did her best to keep her knees decorously together. She held a briefcase in her lap. She pursed her crimson mouth, as if it opened only to eat or speak, and then with discretion. Her fingers were long and tapering; she pressed them together until they were bloodless, and she had filed her nails prudently square. She even went without rouge. But what was the use? Whatever she did to herself she remained beautiful, and looked more like a mistress than a secretary. Keep her eyes downcast as she might, whenever she raised them it could be seen that she was everyone's and anyone's. So she did not expect to deceive guests and members of the Shrapnel Academy for long as to the true nature of her relationship with the General – but was prepared, for his sake, to try to do so. She was as fond of him as she had ever been of anyone. Over seventy he might be, but Bella had never been averse to the love of old men. She generated her own desire: the limbs and lips of young or old would do for her.

In the briefcase were the notes for the General's lecture and, should Bella pall, some whisky for his further pleasure and some magazines for his further entertainment. The whisky was Laphroaig and the magazines included *Fortune*, *Fealty*, *Nature* and *Insignia*, this last distributed free by American Express to those with half-way decent credit ratings. On its heavy pages were advertisements for the most expensive cars in the world, accounts of gourmet dinners in spectacular places and photographs of thin model-girls vivid against Ethiopian sands. Readers were not so much expected to buy, or share, or wear: as to remember that the rewards of the world are always there and worth the fighting for. Theirs not to wonder why, theirs just to do and buy! Zoom! Whee! Is that a missile I see before me? Reader, you will have to forgive me. You know what fiction is; it will keep bursting over into real life, and vice versa.

8

'Bella,' said the General, loudly, into the baffling silence – he meant to speak softly, but at seventy it is sometimes difficult to control the vocal chords – 'you will have your own room at the Academy, being a member of my staff, but you will come and visit me tonight, won't you, and be kind to me?'

'Of course,' she said. That was what she was there for. Everyone needs someone to be kind to them: in a perfect world we should all take turns, giving and receiving kindness. Bella's voice was soft and low, her lips were thin: her outside and her inside only narrowly divided, so that an approach to the outside implied sudden violent access to the inside. The General's hand tightened on her knee: the sinews from his knuckles to his wrist stood out taut and mauve, strong raised highways above pale valleys and dips of papery skin – his fingers hooked beneath her tight black skirt and pulled the fabric up her widening thighs so she feared a seam might fray and split; he elbowed the briefcase onto the floor, and pushed her back upon the velvety seat, and struggled and heaved with her flesh and his own, his khaki gaberdine and her secretarial crimplene much embarrassing them both – and so they travelled down to the Shrapnel Academy – General Leo Makeshift and Bella Morthampton.

Ivor the blond chauffeur adjusted his driving mirror so that he could no longer see what was happening on the other side of the glass partition. So much any good chauffeur should do. Then he switched off the microphone which enabled sound to travel from the back of the car to the front. This too was no more than his professional duty. He could not see, he could not hear, but still he knew, and was disconcerted.

Once Ivor too had taken his pleasure with Bella. She had worked at the cash-desk of the Ministry of Defence staff canteen. He was eighteen; it was five years ago. At the annual staff party he and Bella had drunk together, danced together and spent the night together, making love together in one of the secret cipher rooms. Or he thought they had. But the very next day she had seemed not to recognise him.

She had sat composed and tidy at the canteen cash-desk, seemingly unmarked by the night's experience. Her cheek was smooth and her eyes clear.
'Bella! Bella, it's me!' She raised her large grey eyes to his.
'I'm sorry. Should I know you?'
'But it's me!' he said. He felt like a child knocking at its mother's door and no one answering.
'Of course it's *you*,' she said then, brightly and briskly. 'Everyone is always *them*. 10p for the coffee and 7p the Chelsea Bun.' (The canteen was heavily subsidised.)
He had her bite marks on his shoulders. Whenever he turned his head they hurt. He had woken to the pleasure of these wounds of love. She smiled at him now – yes, those were her teeth, pale and strong – and the amiability of her look belied the cruelty of her words, as she denied him.

'I think you've mistaken me for someone else. Perhaps you only dreamed whatever it was you dreamed? Perhaps someone else said they were me? So many things can happen in this life, especially at night!'

Ivor did not go back to the canteen for a long time and when he did a girl called Debbie-Anne sat in Bella's place. Presently Ivor courted and married Debbie-Anne, and was now father to three children under four, and his wife lay quiet and still beneath him, and let him get on with what he felt he had to do, but did not wrap her legs around his neck as Bella Morthampton had done on the night of the staff party. This is no criticism of Debbie-Anne, reader. It's just that she needed all her strength for her unborn or suckling children. Three children under four is a lot to cope with! Bella, of course, had no children. She didn't like them.

Now Bella was in the back of his car with the General, wrapping her legs where she felt inclined. His one-night stand, the General's mistress! Ivor admired the General while despising Bella, and hoped that when he, Ivor, was seventy, he would still be in such good condition. But of course, it is young men's blood which keeps generals young and virile, and where was Ivor to get a supply of that? Generals are not just anyone; don't think they are. The roads they travel are muddy, and the mud is mixed with blood. Jump out of the way as the limousine rolls by!

Ivor switched the microphone back on. Bella still moaned and the General groaned. It was indecent: but of course it was exciting, as the indecent is. Ivor turned the switch off again, out of respect to Debbie-Anne, and did his best to keep his mind on the road.

The black car was no longer sleek, but mud-spattered. The wipers drove sludge into the corners of the windscreen. Ivor was not sorry. He could spend the weekend cleaning and polishing. Boredom is the occupational hazard of the Ministry chauffeur, waiting in this Rolls or that Mercedes, outside barracks or the palace or on the periphery of parade grounds. Chauffeurs wait, the wrong side of lighted windows, and while they wait they brood.

A right, another right, over a hump-backed bridge, a sharp left along a rutted lane – bump, bump; past a hitchhiker – man or woman, hard to tell which, but in any case ignored. The General and Bella disentwined themselves. Ivor switched on the intercom. Now they travelled narrow lines between high, untrimmed, dripping hedges.

'Nearly there, sir,' said Ivor. He had memorised the map. It was his special talent, and his pride so to do. They passed between tall gates, guarded by a gate-house, down a wide, lit drive lined with trees which no doubt in summer were gracious and majestic, but now were merely sodden and untidy, and there spot-lit, as if waiting for a son-et-lumière performance to begin, stood the Shrapnel Academy, as it had stood for a hundred years, looking for all the world like a scaled-down Buckingham Palace: stout, stone-faced and determinedly grand, in spite of having been badly placed, by its architect, where the ground fell. (It is all very well for a cottage to nestle, but a country house can only properly be at home on rising ground.) Eight great windows ranged on either side of a pillar-flanked front door; twelve smaller ones were ranged above, another row likewise, and then twenty-four little dormer windows stared out from beneath the cornice of the roof. The flagpole was the proud focus of a host of spotlights. From it flew the house flag. This was in yellow silk and embroidered in red upon it were the words THE SHRAPNEL ACADEMY. In the top right-hand corner was a strange device, half-way between an orange and a crown, from which burst streams of light.

'What's the flag?' asked Bella.

'It is the flag of the Shrapnel Academy,' explained the General. 'Always good to see it!'

'What's that thing like a rising sun? Is it the Japanese flag?'

'That is not a rising sun,' he said, a little stiffly. 'What you see there is an exploding cannonball. Henry Shrapnel was its inventor, back in 1804; the Shrapnel Academy is a teaching institution: over the years it has become a shrine to the ethos of military excellence.'

'What a nice gesture,' said Bella. 'Who pays?'

'It is kept going,' said the General, 'by voluntary subscription.'

A few flakes of snow had begun to fall. The flag stopped waving and hung limply. Ivor held a large black umbrella for his passengers and escorted them to the front door – the small, lively General and the tall, pale, beautiful girl.

3

Shirley came down for the Wellington Weekend in the company of her husband Victor, and her children Serena (aged 6), Piers (aged 4) and Nell (aged 3). They travelled in a white Volvo Estate. The dog Harry sat behind a wire mesh and stared out of the back window. Shirley drove. The children slept. Victor dozed. He chose to use his spare time constructively. He needed rest. He had recently been promoted Chief Executive of the Chewinox Division of Gloabal Products Inc. There was a lot to be done: his new broom had to sweep briskly. There were factories to be re-deployed, lay-offs declared, non-aspirers fired, product images re-created, output minimised, profit maximised. His sweeping wrist got tired. Victor slept whenever opportunity arose. He looked like Rock Hudson in his prime: all charm and excellent physique. His daughters adored him. So did his wife. His son sulked. 'He's just like Napoleon,' Shirley would say. 'Able to catnap wherever and whenever.'

Just like Napoleon, pushing out the bounds of empire, drawing the bold red circle of mayhem on the map, so that those inside could wax fat and sleek and safe! And for those outside, who cared? Do you, reader?

Victor and Shirley, and the little Blades, came in response to an invitation. It had arrived a month ago, with the Christmas cards. It came from Joan Lumb and asked the Blades to attend the Wellington Lecture, to be delivered by General Leo Makeshift on January 18th. Joan Lumb was Victor's eldest sister. She, a colonel's widow, had been made Custodian/Administrator of the Shrapnel Academy two years previously. It was a much coveted post, now for the first time given to a woman. The honour was self-evident.

'Does she mean us to pay?' asked Shirley. There was a handwritten letter with the card. She handed both now to Victor.

'Don't just come for the lecture,' Joan Lumb had written in her big bold handwriting. 'Come for the whole weekend! We're having an Eve-of-Waterloo dinner on the Friday. The menu's very special – a real surprise. We've a full house for the lecture already. Two hundred of the great and good from the ends of the earth. Not surprising, I suppose: the General's a splendid speaker and a real world figure, even in peace time. Stay for Sunday if you can. I know Shirley can't bear to be away from home, but we are family, aren't we, and I haven't seen either of you for so long. We're between courses here – the Westpoint and St Cyr lads have gone and the Sandhurst Refresher week's not started, so you can take your choice of rooms. I've provisionally booked you the Napoleon Suite: over the West Porch with a view over the ornamental gardens. So pretty in this bright, frosty weather. A real bargain at £35, I always think!'

'I don't know,' said Victor, handing back the letter, 'whether or not she expects us to pay. I leave that kind of thing to you.'

'I suppose we have to go?' asked Shirley.

'We do,' he said. Victor and Joan's parents were dead. Joan was all Victor had left of his past; Shirley and the children were his present and his future, but a man must have his past as well, if he is to be whole, no matter how much he dislikes it.

'What about the children?' asked Shirley. 'She doesn't mention the children. Does she mean us to bring them?'

'I don't suppose,' said Victor, 'that the Shrapnel Academy often rings to the sound of children's voices, but you must decide.'

'Well,' said Shirley, 'I'll see what I can manage by way of babysitters. But I don't know if I'll have any luck.'

'I dread to think what the special menu is,' said Victor. 'Probably what the officers ate on the eve of Waterloo. Greasy and fattening.'

'So long as it isn't what the men ate,' said Shirley. 'Because that would be dry bread and maggots.'

'I hardly think it was as bad as that,' said Victor, rather curtly. 'An army always looks after its own.' Victor came from an army family, who, although happy enough to attack the army themselves, did not like outsiders to do so. Victor had formally renounced the army and gone into business, but who can renounce such an upbringing? Its ethics run in the blood, not the brain. Revulsion is only skin deep.

'Is that a rising sun on the invitation?' asked Shirley brightly and pacifically, to change the subject. Shirley's parents had been teachers, and socialists. That too runs in the blood, not the mind. Hers and Victor's had been a love-match, and a cause of anxiety to both sets of parents.

'No,' said Victor. 'I imagine that is the symbol of the Shrapnel Academy. Henry Shrapnel invented the exploding cannonball in 1804.'

'What did he do that for?' asked Shirley. She liked to ask Victor questions, and he liked to answer them.

'To gain promotion and be hailed as a genius,' said Victor. 'Why does anyone do anything?'

'I see,' said Shirley, dutifully. Presently, having thought a little, she added, 'I suppose it's better to bring a war to an end quickly, even if nastily. Otherwise it just lingers on and demoralises everyone. Was that the thinking behind the exploding cannonball, Victor?'

But for once he did not reply. He was catnapping again, between the last sips of breakfast coffee and the arrival of the company car. That day he was to cut the proportion of gum in Chewinox by one part in a thousand. Twelve villages in Southern India would die.

The invitation was accepted, the Napoleon Suite booked and no mention of money made. Shirley made babysitting arrangements and Victor returned home early, at 3.25 on the Friday afternoon. As he changed out of his grey stubbly-woven heavy silk suit into more deliberately casual weekend clothes, he said: 'I wish we were taking the children. I don't see enough of them as it is.'

'We are taking them,' said Shirley. 'We have to. Angie left this morning. She walked out after breakfast.'

'Why?'

'She threw away Piers' comforter,' said Shirley, 'saying he was too old for it. And he bit her.'

'Good for Piers.'

'That was my reaction,' said Shirley, 'and I said so. So she got upset. I would have been more sympathetic, I expect, had I liked her. But I didn't, I'm sorry to say. Nor did the children. All in all I'm glad she's gone.'

'So am I!' he said. 'Our lives to ourselves again! Just the five of us, two big and three small.' Victor loved his family, his present and his future, wrapped safely into one; so much better than the past.

'They'll sleep in the car,' said Shirley. 'They've fizzed and overflowed all day they're so glad she's gone. Now they're flat and calm and tired.'

'Like Asti Spumanti,' he said, dreamily, 'opened for an hour or two.' They took their holidays in Italy, their happiness thus being complete.

'Do you think Joan will mind very much,' asked Shirley, 'if we bring them?'

'Joan will just have to put up with them,' said Victor.

The moods and fears of unmarried, childless and no longer young women are easily disregarded by those in the active, fruitful and positive mainstream of their lives. I hope, for your sake, reader, you belong to this latter group. But do remember that membership of it is only temporary: so try to be less ruthless than Victor and Shirley.

Serena, Piers and Nell were put in the back of the car while their parents locked up the house, a process which of necessity took some time. Harry the Doberman took up his position behind the dog mesh. The children heaved and fought for a little, as they liked to do, and then fell obligingly asleep in a warm tangle of limbs. Harry trembled and waited. The house had been recently re-protected by security experts to the high standard required for Chief Executives at Gloabal. Victor, on leaving, threw a master switch too soon and locked himself in and Shirley out. Internal sensors detected the presence of an intruder. Sirens went off in the garage, waking and frightening the children, and Harry, who rolled his eyes and slavered at the mouth. Red lights flashed at the Police Station. Shirley soothed the children, and fed one of her tranquillisers to Harry. Victor, unable to nullify his last security decision, now electronically enforced, waited in the kitchen, while the police summoned the Gloabal Security Officer. He, on arrival, first checked Victor's voice patterns against a master, and then talked the system down with his own voice, to which the relays were programmed to respond. Victor was released, and the police went home. 'Think nothing of it, sir,' said the Security Officer. 'It's what I'm paid for.'

When they finally set off, an hour late, Shirley said, 'It's wonderful to know the system works, and feel so safe. Gloabal certainly knows how to look after its employees! Aren't you glad you work for them?'

But Victor was catnapping again, gathering strength. Shirley left the blueness of the motorway for the yellowness of a minor road, for the modest white double line of a country lane. In the back the children sucked happily on bottles, between sleep and drowsiness. Victor smiled as he napped. Occasional flakes of snow hit the windscreen. Shirley was happy. She drove as fast as the various roads allowed. She made good time. Her headlights picked out a hitchhiker – a young woman in jeans and donkey jacket, with a rucksack in her hand. Perhaps she should stop? What was a girl doing here, so far from anywhere, and in the dark? Shirley drove on. No. If that was the sort of situation a girl could get into, that was the sort she could get out of, without expecting big white passing Volvo Estates, full of husbands, children, cases, dogs, to stop. Some shabby vehicle of the kind Shirley's parents once had owned, would stagger along presently, flaking rust, and like would call to like, and help would be at hand.

And so, in tune with their prosperity, and their virtue, made only a little late by the problems that accompany success and power, Shirley, Victor, and the little Blades approached the Shrapnel Academy: Shirley driving, the children sleeping, Victor dozing, and Harry the dog, the sleek black Doberman, quivering in surprise as snow swirled out of the darkness to hit the heated rear window, where it melted and disappeared. There one minute, gone the next! Harry was less than a year old and had never seen snow before. He did not like surprises.

4

Baf drove a dark green sportscar: it scuttled between the high hedges as if it were a beetle running for cover. Baf had owned the car for a week. It was thirty years old, two years older than blond Baf himself. There was a map-light attachment on the dashboard and a compass stuck by suction to the windscreen. Baf drove with the roof open, regardless of the cold. He wore a leather flying jacket with a fur collar, turned up high beneath his square and handsome jaw. He was in a hurry to see Muffin, who worked at the Shrapnel Academy. Muffin was Joan Lumb's secretary. Baf had visited the Academy, in secret, many times. He would telephone ahead, so Muffin would be watching the drive when he arrived. She would open one of the side doors for her lover. They would hurry up the back-stairs to her small bedroom on the third floor where he would throw himself upon her, leaving her scarcely any time at all to remove her garments. The red horse-heads upon her royal blue headscarf and his fur collar were etched into the other's erotic consciousness.

Reader, what is etched in yours? What collar-bone, what little patch of textured skin, what dangling pendant? Think! Remember! Keep back the glacier of age by the sheer warmth, the sheer force of sexual recollections, wild imaginings! It can be done: it is worth the doing.

Today Baf would go to the front door, openly. He too had been invited by Joan Lumb to come to dinner and meet the General. The dinner would no doubt be boring, but Baf would at least stay overnight, officially. Muffin would have the sense to put him in a room easily accessible to hers. And Baf would take the opportunity, during the Saturday morning, of cornering the General and demonstrating the miniaturised weaponry he carried in a velvet-lined Victorian knife box in the boot of the car. Once such fire power would have needed a half-mile wagon train to carry it. Now, a knife box! Oh, nifty! Oh, progress! Stunning! Oh, the cleverness of men! Bump, goes the knife box the other side of a hump-backed bridge. Up, down, bump, and bump again.

Baf did not think he would marry Muffin. Someone better would probably come along: Kashoggi's daughter, Arafat's niece. And Muffin, to be fair, felt that marriage to Baf was likewise unsuitable. One married, she supposed, for a quiet life. Sooner or later, Muffin expected to be the wife of one of the young officers who came to the Shrapnel Academy for courses in Weapons Through the Ages, The Rule of Law, The Concept of the Just War, and so forth. She also sometimes thought, regretfully, that it probably wouldn't make much difference which one it was. They all seemed much the same: that is to say, shy and sweet, rather like Muffin herself. If she smiled at them, they would smile shyly and sweetly back, but she had to smile first. Muffin was spectacularly long-legged and shaggy-headed: she had large blue eyes with droopy lids. She seemed to inspire romantic rather than erotic love in the hearts of young men other than Baf. If she dropped a drawing-pin, when pinning lists and rotas on the noticeboards, there would be a dive to the rescue, and a trembling of hands if hers touched theirs. Well, that was right. Husbands should respect wives. And Baf didn't respect Muffin; she could tell by the things he did in bed. Muffin thought she would just put off marriage as long as she possibly could. But how the gentle, soulful young cadets were ever to become men of war, she could not imagine: storm towns and drop bombs and so on!

Baf realised that the bump and lurch after the hump-backed bridge, which he had rather enjoyed, was unfamiliar. He had taken a wrong turning, an easy enough thing to do in such a spiderweb of lanes: the light snow which was now falling blanked out detail and made one crossroads much like another. He stopped at the next signposted turning, took out the map and switched on the map-light, pleased to have found an opportunity for making use of it. The compass, alas, had fallen off the windscreen. Baf located it on the floor, re-licked its suckers, and pressed it on again. It stayed. A right turn and then another should, he imagined, after proper consultation of map and compass, bring him back to familiar territory. So he had planned his route in the past, in the uncharted wastes of the Sahara, and in jungle tracks in Bolivia and over the South African veldt. A compass had never fallen off before. He imagined it was the cold and damp which did it.

After the first right turn his headlights picked out a motor-bike lying by the side of the hedged road. He slowed, thinking perhaps there had been an accident. He saw no signs of a body, but after the next turn came upon a young woman, walking away from him in the centre of the narrow road. She carried a rucksack in one hand, and a bike helmet in the other. When she heard the car, she pressed herself against the hedge to let it pass. Baf slowed, stopped, lowered the window. There was not much of her to be seen, inasmuch as a donkey jacket concealed her figure, and her head was wrapped in a long woolly scarf, of the kind he had so often seen on Jumble Sale stalls in his youth, when his mother had been active raising funds for the Little Sisters of Mercy Overseas. But she was young, female, in trouble and he wished to help.

'Can I give you a lift?'
'No, you cannot.'
The reply was curt: the tone of voice almost offensive. Baf was hurt. He noticed, so bright was the map-light which he now switched on, that she was wearing heavy boots and that their laces were double-knotted. He had the feeling that if he pressed the matter she might well produce a knife and use it. She was the kind of young woman who carried cartons of pepper to throw in men's eyes, and handy pocket tear-gas

sprays to blind them. Then when the man was helpless, weeping and coughing, and no doubt deafened by an alarm siren as well, she would get him with the boots. Girls like that were everywhere, these days. Baf wound up the window, and carried on. Let her walk. Muffin, in similar circumstances, would have accepted a lift. Those who looked for evil found none, and Baf had certainly meant none. He was glad to notice it was snowing harder, as he turned into the grounds of the Shrapnel Academy.

5

Murray Fairchild, discovering there was no bus service, was obliged to take a taxi to the Academy from the station at Stupehampton; a distance of fourteen miles. He thought Joan Lumb should have warned him of the expense.

'The Shrapnel Academy? They say they make nerve gas in there,' said the driver, settling in for a chat. Murray wanted only silence. The driver was a middle-aged woman. She chain-smoked. She had a bad head cold.
'Of course that's only silly rumour, but what does go on there? Or is it secret?'
'It isn't secret,' said Murray. He spoke courteously, in spite of his irritation. He who had deflected bullets in Vietnam, withstood torture in Argentina, and narrowly escaped defenestration in Pakistan, found difficulty in being impolite to women. 'The Shrapnel Academy is similar to an Arts Centre, but military in its nature.'
'Oh, I see,' she said. He doubted that she did.

He stretched his right leg. It ached, and it itched. There was, he knew, a tracery of engorged veins between ankle and knee. The whole leg, were he to look, would have a curiously mottled red and mauve appearance. Yet his left leg remained smooth, lean and bronze. He was sixty. Various physical changes were to be expected with the years, but why should the passage of time affect the right leg, and not the left?
'Something the matter with your leg?' she asked.
'No.'
'Bet there is. You men are all the same. Take it to the doctor before it's too late.'
'Thank you for your advice,' he said. But he did not mean

to take it. No hypochondriac he, to go running to doctors. A sprinkling of antibiotic powder on a jungle sore, some quinine for malaria, a plank for a slipped disc – Murray did his own doctoring. The leg would respond to healthy living, positive thinking, in its own good time.

'So, what's your business at the Shrapnel Academy?'

'I'm a guest there,' he said, shortly. He was to be the lion at Joan Lumb's dinner party. People would know who he was, and have the politeness not to talk about it. He wished that life could be lived without words, or at worst captions. Wham! Whee! Take that, and that! Ouch! Ugh! And the final dying Cr-cr-croak!

He wished he had chosen any other taxi than this.

'You look like James Bond, only twenty years on,' she observed. 'Is that your line of business?' She coughed and spluttered. He would need to take Vitamin C tablets as soon as possible.

'Don't usually find a man like you taking a taxi,' she said, when her nasal passages were more composed. 'What happened? Lose your licence? Driving under the influence?'

It was true that Murray had been disqualified from driving, on the grounds of drunkenness, many times, in many courts and in many lands. But if he wanted to drive, he drove, licensed or not. It was the ache in his right leg which now disqualified him as a driver, more effectively than any police force had ever managed, and obliged him to take taxis and put up with the inquisitions of strangers. He would as soon, he thought, step into a Khmer Rouge camp by night as into a taxi with a sneezing woman driver.

'Hit the nail on the head, then!' she remarked, when he did not reply. They were within a mile or so of the Shrapnel Academy when they approached a hitchhiker.

'Don't pull up,' he said, sharply.

Once, years ago, he had stopped for a young woman, apparently involved in an accident on a Route Nationale.

25

Out of the damaged car had stepped two armed men. Murray had been taken hostage, held for ransom, confined in a small space and it was four months before he was able to escape. Now he came to think of it, it was probably that particular confinement, that lack of exercise, which had started the trouble with his leg. He seemed to remember a sharp blow on the right knee-cap. With the remembrance came a twinge. 'Don't stop,' he repeated, but the woman simply ignored him and pulled up alongside the hitchhiker. And there were bars in Agadir where men melted away at Murray's approach!

'Where do you want to go?' the woman driver asked.

'The Shrapnel Academy.' It was a girl. Her face was muffled against the cold, but he thought the eyes had the steady, careful, haunted look of the female terrorist.

'Drive on!' he said, and the pain in his knee stabbed sharply.

'I'll just drop this fare off,' said the driver to the girl, 'since he's so nervous. Then I'll come back and give you a lift.'

'I'd be grateful,' said the girl, and they left her standing on the side of the road and she became part of the darkness of the past.

'Naughty, naughty, paranoia!' said the taxi driver to Murray.

Democracy, thought Murray, was scarcely worth preserving, or the personal freedoms which went with it, since it was preserved for the likes of the woman taxi driver, who could only abuse all possible freedoms.

'Penny for your thoughts!'

He ignored her.

'My, you are a deep one. I bet they do make poison gas up there.'

'There it is ahead!' she said, as the gates of the Shrapnel Academy appeared. 'Bhopal, we call it, down on the rank. We got there just before the weather. They really get snowed in up here! You'll be lucky to get out before March. Or have you brought your skis?'

'You can see I have no skis,' he said. She was a very stupid woman.

'You might have the new lightweight collapsible ones tucked away in your pocket, for all I know.'

Murray did not think any such new style of skis existed. He would have heard. He'd skied across the Spanish border into France during the war, a dozen times or so. The skis themselves were always the main problem. How to dispose of them? Now if he could have put them in his pocket – but then where would have been the peril, where the point?

'Only joking,' she said. She charged him half what he had anticipated. He had the same sudden feeling of elation as once, when he was twelve, his mother had given him twice his normal weekly pocket money, by mistake. He went almost jauntily up the steps, and almost without limping, a thick-set, grizzled man with a wide brow, slightly brain-damaged by various blows to his head over a long period, deep eyes and a kindly manner, and hands adept at taking life, but only, ever, for the sake of principle, never inclination.

6

Edna the taxi driver returned to pick up the hitchhiker. She did so out of simple kindness, and in no expectation of reward. The night was dark, the girl was young.

'Silly old fart,' she said of her last customer.

The girl unwound her yellow and brown knitted scarf in the warmth of the car. She had a lean, young face, stern rather than pretty, quick blue eyes and frizzed out hair of no particular colour. She said her name was Medusa, but people called her Mew.

'That's a funny name,' said Edna.

The girl explained that her mother had been a Greek scholar who took the view that Medusa was Jason's victim, and that serving him his own children in a pie was no less than he deserved. The mother had called her daughter after her favourite person.

'I see,' said Edna. But Mew thought she probably didn't. Mew's mother was a feminist. That too runs in the blood, not the brain.

'My poor mother,' said Mew. 'They put her in a nut house, in the end. And it wasn't even as if she got Medusa right. Jason's girlfriend was Medea. Is it far to the Academy? I ran out of petrol.'

'A couple of miles,' said Edna. 'But I'll take you for free. No skin off my nose. What's your business at Shrapnel?' It was a puzzle. The girl was white, and so was hardly likely to be on the domestic staff of the Shrapnel Academy. And not having the gloss that money and power gives, she could hardly be a guest: nor could she be one of the students, for they were always male: nor one of the teaching staff, for they spoke with the soft authority of the privileged classes. This girl's voice had a workaday, anxious twang.

'I'm a journalist,' said the girl. 'Someone's making a speech there tomorrow. Some general.'

Edna did not believe her. This was not, in her experience, how journalists looked and behaved. They did not wind themselves in woolly scarves, ride motorbikes and run out of petrol.

'You don't believe me,' said the girl, 'but it's true. I'm on the staff of the *Woman's Times*. It's a new daily newspaper. Feminist. Have you heard of it?'

Edna hadn't. How fast the world changed. One moment women stayed at home and baked steak and kidney pie; the next they drove taxis, published newspapers, and beef was bad for you and pastry worse.

'If you give me your address,' said Mew, 'I'll send you a copy of the *Times*. You really ought to read it. Every woman should. It will explain so much to you!'

Edna said she knew more than enough already. She sneezed and eased out a damp tissue from beneath the cuff of her sleeve and dabbed at her nose, which was bright pink and painful around the nostrils. She changed her mind and tucked back the tissue and sniffed up instead; it hurt less and was more efficacious, if noisier, and the girl was getting a free ride.

'Is that it?' asked the girl in alarm, when she saw the spotlit splendour of the Academy, and its flag flying proudly through the blizzard. She had assumed, on accepting the assignment, that she would be visiting some local College of Further Education, tucked somewhere at the back of a High Street in a country town. Mew had not envisaged anything so grand, nor anywhere so remote as this. She knew nothing about the army. How could she? Why should she?

'That's it,' said Edna. 'That's the Shrapnel Academy, and thank God for it. It keeps the taxi-rank in business. We'd all be bankrupt otherwise.'

The taxi's wheels stuck and spun in soft snow as Edna

reversed and set off home. The sky was clearing; she could even see a star sparkling above the trees. If the snow stopped falling and then froze on the ground, and then started again, as the weather forecast suggested, there would be a hard weekend ahead on the roads.

7

Through that afternoon the Shrapnel Academy prepared itself for the Wellington Weekend. The Eve-of-Waterloo dinner was the least of its problems. That was to be an *intime* affair, with merely twelve around the table, to be served in the panelled dining-room, not the gold-encrusted banqueting hall. But two hundred were expected for the Wellington Lecture on the Saturday afternoon, and to celebrate the event later at the traditional Tea. In the kitchen teams of servants had been preparing smoked salmon (Canadian), mushroom vol-au-vents (using canned Cuban mushrooms), cucumber and tomato sandwiches (these from Israel), strawberries (fresh from Australia) and cream (local), and tropical fruit salad from the equatorial regions. A splendid chocolate-and-rum gâteau was yet to be prepared, from a copy of *Recipes for New Zealand Teas* given to Joan Lumb on her twenty-first birthday by an antipodean aunt. What a wonderful place the world is today: no one need fear winter, when summer is only flight-hours away! There would not be muffins for tea: Joan Lumb, the Administrator, did not think at all highly of Rupert Brooke's poetry. She had not read it, but knew from hearsay she would not like it, and in this her judgement was quite right. She had embarrassed Victor greatly by claiming on his wedding day that 'If' was her favourite poem, and after 'If' – 'Trees'.

> Poems are made by fools like me,
> But only God can make a tree.

'Pity he didn't try a bit harder with the elm,' said Victor, 'and make it impervious to Dutch Elm Disease.' Really, the two of them did not get on. It was a source of sorrow to them both. They were orphaned brother and sister, and should have gone hand in hand, in a perfect world.

Joan Lumb summonsed Muffin from the administration offices, where she was trying to make the word processor allocate rooms on a non-random basis to the seventy-five guests who planned to stay on after the Waterloo Ball on the Saturday night. She needed help, Joan Lumb said, in setting the eleven name places for the Dinner Intime in the dining-room.

'So important,' said Joan Lumb, 'to get the seating arrangements right. A dinner party's like a cocktail – no matter how good the ingredients, if you don't stir properly, everything's wasted.'

She and Muffin stood in the dining-room, while the grandfather clock ticked by the minutes until the guests arrived. Muffin fidgeted, while Joan Lumb put a card here, then changed it for one there, and then stood back to admire the effect, as a stage designer might, the better to admire the efficacy of a set. So much to be done, so little time to do it! But employers are like that: they can seldom, in the employee's eyes, distinguish the unimportant from the important.

The dining-room was long and low, the walls panelled in Victorian oak. The room should have been handsome, but was not. The sideboards were good pieces, the chairs valuable, but were out of sorts with each other. A central crystal chandelier which would have done well enough in a higher, squarer room, in this one cast uneasy shadows. Faded tapestries lined the walls: they had little merit except age. The archers of Agincourt, the hosts of Thermopylae, the vengeance of Marathon, the fury of Saratoga, all fading gently into the past, stitched long ago by docile female hands, the widows and orphans of the warrior race. Who else but the unlucky sew for a living? And how else but by glorifying the abysmal, can we make the abysmal glorious? The sewers stitched, no doubt, with loving hands, and worshipped their oppressors.

Joan Lumb wore a brown tweed skirt (size 18), and a cream woollen blouse (size 12), brown stockings and rather surprising bright yellow shoes (size 8) with white bows. Her hair, which was brown to grey and usually plainly and sensibly washed and dried, had today been put in curlers, and was now arranged in elegant sweeps and curls about her beak-nosed face. She would, of course, change before dinner, before Murray came.

The sight, indeed even the thought, of Murray made Joan Lumb's heart beat faster, made her swallow, made her moisten her lips, made her voice rise to a higher pitch. These are the physical effects of love. Where else but in such a man could Joan Lumb find her match? Brave Murray, lonely Murray, steadfast Murray, bearing alone the intolerable burden of secrecy, slipping by stealth out of this country, into that, facing torture, imprisonment, ignominy, death; organising, resisting, linking this cell, that cell, joining together men and women of goodwill, in the secret fight against barbarism, godlessness. Murray was employed sometimes by the CIA, sometimes by MI5, sometimes by more enigmatic folk; but all of whom loved freedom, hated oppression. Others talked, Murray *did*. Joan Lumb looked into the hearts of other men and saw there poverty, vacillation and shoddiness – a sorry incapacity for fine deeds and a frightening lack of noble aspiration. What was happening to mankind? The past was littered with glorious empires; strewn with great men, heroic deeds – now there was nothing but self-doubt, cowardly words, pacifism, lack of resolve. Only in Murray the man did Joan Lumb catch a glimpse of the greatness which had so illuminated the past. She would die for him, she thought, just as he would die for a cause he believed in. Well, that was woman's part. They were the hero's recreation and his inspiration. She wished she had been born a man. Her brother Victor should have been the girl, she the boy.

'I was afraid there was going to be a real male–female imbalance,' Joan Lumb said brightly to Muffin. 'That's the only trouble with the army: so many more men than women when it comes to dinner parties!'

(You have your troubles, Joan Lumb, I have mine!)

Muffin wore jeans and sneakers and a fluffy green sweater, which made her blue eyes bluer and her fair hair fairer; her bra did not properly contain her bust. Joan Lumb wished Muffin would hurry up and get married, so she could employ someone smaller and neater. She had taken on Muffin for Muffin's father's sake, when he was handling the estate of her late husband, Lieutenant-Colonel Sir Aubrey Lumb. Muffin's father had proved drunk and incompetent; the estate yielded a quarter of the amount it should; she had taken her business elsewhere and still she was landed with Muffin, who ate more food than was reasonable, and kept her electric blanket on all night, and treated the Academy word-processor as if it could think for itself, which only a fool would do.

'I wish you wouldn't wear jeans,' said Joan Lumb. 'If a woman isn't a proper woman, how can a man be a proper man? Surely this is the root of many of today's troubles!'
'My jersey's fluffy,' said Muffin. 'Won't that make up for it?'
'Good heavens,' said Joan, 'by a proper woman I don't mean someone fluffy. I mean someone with dignity and proper standards.'
'Well, anyway,' said Muffin, 'I'm changing for dinner. Nobody can see.'
'God can see,' said Joan Lumb, 'and I can see you. And the servants, most certainly, can see.'

Oh, they saw, they saw! The Shrapnel Academy employed a host of servants of every race except Caucasian. They came as supplicants from India, Pakistan, Mexico, Indonesia, Puerto Rico, Sri Lanka, Cuba, Nicaragua, seeking shelter, food, employment. Few had visas which would stand careful inspection. Behind them they left parents, spouses, children, friends: each life a reproach to a wicked God, the God that Joan Lumb loved. They saw, they watched, they waited! Dark eyes glowed, bright or sombre, sulky or docile, watching and observing, but what sense did they make of what they saw? Did they so much as include Muffin in the human-race? This untidily bodied white woman who left her dirty knickers on the floor and her soiled Tampax in the bin? (She couldn't use the WC. Notices saying 'Disposable does not mean flushable' could not forever be ignored.) This young woman who fornicated freely with her secret lover, at all times of day or night, without ritual, without shame, like an animal? It could hardly matter how she clothed her legs, she was so far beyond disgrace. Yet they admired her, how could they not; the unbearably privileged are much admired: admiration is a healing emotion. Why else do the elderly die of hypothermia blessing the Queen? the soldier expire from his wounds whilst praising his general? Admiration of the lucky! Luck, luck: luck is the God of the luckless. Muffin was lucky. The servants were not. How could they not admire her, even while they despised her?

What are we to do? What, as Lenin asked, is to be *Done*? Why, get on with the story.

'I should never have asked the girl from *The Times*,' said Joan Lumb. 'I did it on impulse. But that's me all over – impulsive!' She misjudged herself, but who doesn't?
'Her voice on the telephone,' Joan Lumb complained, 'was not at all promising. No girl of good family talks like that.'
On hearing from Muffin that the Features Editor of *The Times* was on the phone, Joan Lumb had grabbed the instrument in her eagerness to talk.
'It's quite trendy,' said Muffin, 'not to talk posh even if you are.'
'Not with that particular nasal twang,' said Joan Lumb. 'No, she comes from the Inner City. She simply won't fit in. She will be ever so intellectual and ever so plain. I should never have asked her. Who will I sit her next to? What a puzzle!'

35

'So long as she doesn't knock the General in the interview,' said Muffin, 'I don't suppose it matters.'

'My dear Muffin,' said Joan Lumb, 'I hardly imagine *The Times* has been infiltrated by beatniks, peaceniks and subversives. You do have a brain, I suppose. Please use it!' Muffin sulked. Joan Lumb didn't notice.

'I have to get back to Room Allocation,' said Muffin. The sooner she finished the more time she would have with Baf. She licked her full lips with her pink tongue.

'Don't *do* that,' said Joan Lumb. 'You'll chap your lips. Now who is this Bella whatsit the General's bringing? Perhaps she could sit next to the girl from *The Times*? Heaven knows what she's like either, or why I should be expected to have her at my dinner table! What's the matter with his wife?'

Let us answer the question for her, since Muffin won't. The very same things that were the matter with Lord Nelson's wife; age and respectability. Emma Hamilton, Nelson's mistress – for there is only very little fairness in this world – got asked almost everywhere. She was always fun, and dressed up, or rather down, after dinner, and did Greek poses on marble tables, prettily and scantily draped. Lady Nelson would never have done a thing like that.

'She's only his secretary,' said Muffin, relenting. 'The General must be over seventy. I've arranged for the chauffeur to have a meal in his room. He might feel awkward in the Servants' Hall.' She meant that he was white and the servants were not. 'If you like, I could arrange for Bella Morthampton to do likewise.'

'I wouldn't want to offend the General in any way,' said Joan. 'This country owes so much to him I'm sure we can overlook a peccadillo or so. He did particularly ask for Bella to sit next to him.'

'Perhaps he needs her to cut up his meat.'

'Perhaps,' said Joan. 'Of course he can't dictate to his hostess and expect to get away with it altogether!'

Muffin perceived that it was unlikely that Bella Mort-

36

hampton would be sat next to the General. And she knew better than to suggest that she should sit next to Baf, or that would never happen either.

Muffin peered out from between the damask curtains. The fabric was a rather dismal faded maroon, braid trimmed. And not gracefully faded, at that, but more as if a host of insect pests had first nibbled and gnawed at the surface and then bleached out the colour by sucking it up as mosquitoes suck blood.

'Supposing we're snowed in. What fun!'

'We can't be,' said Joan Lumb, flatly. 'God wouldn't allow it.'

Muffin went back to her office and the word processor.

8

The telephone rang in Muffin's office. It was Panza Jordan, the tutor in communications, who lived with his computers in the old summer house in the Academy grounds. He was coming to dinner, but wanted more. Give an inch, others will take an ell!

'Muffin,' he said, 'can you fix me up a room in the house for tonight? Snow's forecast; in fact, it's already beginning. If the line comes down, and it may, I don't want to be without electricity. You know how I hate to be cold.'

'Of course,' said Muffin, and told Joan.

'That man's frightened by his own shadow,' said Joan Lumb, who was still changing place names. 'Scared of a little cold and dark! I wouldn't have asked him to dinner either, but I had no option. All he'll do is talk about Artificial Intelligence and bore the pants off everyone. Give him Tiglath-Pileser.'

'I don't think the heating's working properly in Tiglath-Pileser,' said Muffin.

'I've had it seen to,' said Joan Lumb, though Muffin knew well enough she hadn't.

Rooms of any significance in the Shrapnel Academy were named after famous battles, kings or generals. These two latter were often the same thing: it being the custom of hereditary rulers to take over not just the running of the country, but its army as well. Consider the exceptional line of English royal generals – Richard the Lionheart, Edward I, Edward II, the Black Prince, Henry V – all related! Perhaps God had a hand in it? Perhaps the Divine Right of Kings is not to be sneezed at?

38

The Emperor Tiglath-Pileser III came to the Assyrian throne in 745 BC, and is reckoned the first of the military genii. He it was who had the idea of organising the entire state around a permanent regular army. Under his guidance, the principal business of Assyria became war. Its wealth was sustained by booty from plundered neighbours, and its prosperity – which was great – by the general activity engendered by energetically servicing an army. Tiglath-Pileser set about refurbishing his entire army. Out went the iron weapons, in came the bronze! Better, lighter, faster, tougher! It is of great benefit to any nation to introduce new weapons and systematically improve them. Not only does it increase the general prosperity – the creation of work, in any above-subsistence society, creates wealth – and bring about a technical superiority above other nations (at least until they catch up), but keeps the soldiers busy and on their toes, in periods of peace, learning how to use them.

Reader, do not skip. I know you want to. So do I. What has this ancient person to do with anyone? Surely his very name prevents him being taken seriously! Tiglath-Pileser III! But do remember – what went before so very much informs what goes on now. If Joan Lumb and the Management Board of the Shrapnel Academy think the Emperor Tiglath-Pileser warrants a room named after him, albeit neglected and chilly, by God he deserves our attention.

Tiglath-Pileser III lived in the pre-gunpowder age known as the Age of Muscle. In those days you just hit (with a club, or blunt sword) or slashed (with a sharp sword) or pierced (with a pointed sword) or, more safely, hurled heavy rocks or sharp sticks from a distance by means of a sling or bow. You could reckon casualties on an abacus. But Assyria's enemies – and of course Assyria had enemies, even before it started its unpopular scavenging habits. As individuals we have enemies, so how can any State not? The State is only ourselves, writ larger – were naturally sensitive to this development in weapon technique. They had to do better themselves – a yet more supple sword, a yet slimmer

arrow – seeing the process as self-defence and themselves
innocent of any aggressive intent. And Assyria, in its turn,
then felt obliged, for survival's sake, to outdo its enemies.
(The guiltier a nation is, of course, the more paranoic it
feels. Just as an unfaithful husband is all too ready to believe
his wife an adulteress.) This lethal march forward, this
Progress by Weapon, step by innocent step, walking through
the Age of Muscle, running through the Age of Gunpowder,
leaping and bounding through the Age of Technology
towards the Age of Megadeath, was started long ago by
Tiglath-Pileser III, when he had his bright idea and refur-
bished his army with weapons of bronze.

Thank you, Tiglath-Pileser! Hail and farewell!

But hold on a moment, before you go. May we also congratulate you upon your mastery of the politics of terror?
Most armies are cruel enough, and ferocious enough (and
how can they not be, why should they not be, since their
major purpose is the pleasure of sanctified slaughter,) but
you really knew what you were doing. You calculated. When
your troops – and they would march out in armies 50,000
strong – captured a city they would kill everyone in it, every
man, woman and child, in the most disagreeable way they
could think of. Pulling, twisting, wrenching, crushing, sear-
ing. Or, if they needed slaves, they would carry entire
populations away into captivity. The memory lingers on.
You are not forgotten, Emperor Tiglath-Pileser III. At the
going down of the sun we will remember you! Byron helps,
as poets do.

'The Assyrians came down like the wolf on the fold,'

he wrote,

'And their cohorts were gleaming in purple and gold –
And the sheen of their spears
Was like stars on the sea
Where the blue waves roll nightly
On deep Galilee–'

Lovely!

Of course civilisation has come a long way since then, as we shall see, if only in the ingenuity of its weapons. And computers, of course, are needed to measure deaths. You could not conveniently do it on an abacus; you can calculate almost anything on an abacus of course: it just takes a long time. Your own death would intervene before you'd finished the calculation.

9

Sergei Wootton was the next to appeal to Muffin for help. He was the lecturer in Liberal Studies, who had his rooms in the Folly at the bottom of the West Garden. His voice was high and querulous. It was about to snow. He too wanted a room in the house for the night. His light and heating would go off. It had happened before and would happen again.

'Give him Alexander,' said Joan Lumb.

'It's supposed to be haunted,' said Muffin. 'You know how nervous Mr Wootton is!'

'Mr Wootton has no business being nervous,' said Joan Lumb. 'A man who believes in ghosts is not fit to teach our students. There are plenty of others looking for his job if he doesn't want it. Such a pity he's coming to dinner. He'll talk about the library in Alexandria all night and no one will understand a word he's saying. I know Murray simply hates it when people talk about art.'

'I don't believe in ghosts,' said Muffin sensibly, 'but it is true that Alexander has a rather peculiar atmosphere. It's always cold, no matter how you turn up the heating.'

'It's a corner room,' said Joan Lumb briskly. 'There is no room for superstition in the army. At least I had the sense to invite Victor, who is always sensible about everything! Though I'm in two minds about Shirley. She will ask perfect strangers what sign of the Zodiac they were born under. Perhaps I'd better sit her next to Sergei. They can sop up each other's nonsense. But that means you won't be able to sit next to Baf. I expect you want to.'

'Good heavens,' said Muffin prudently, 'I see more than enough of Baf!' Though she didn't, she didn't! She would like to see Baf, be with Baf, thirty-six hours out of every twenty-four, if that could have been managed. 'Anyway,' she added, 'I don't think Alexander's made up.'

'What do we keep servants for,' said Joan Lumb, 'if not to make rooms up. Have it done at once!'

The room Joan Lumb thus decreed for Sergei Wootton was named after Alexander of Macedonia. Macedonia is in today's Northern Greece and part of the Common Market. Alexander, who lived in the third century BC, was another hereditary ruler, and at an amazingly youthful age conquered all the lands around by devising a way of using human beings themselves as weapons – the thundering, powerful, noisy, relentless, invincible, charging Phalanx. This was a flock of running men, in disciplined, tactical formation, its rows eighteen men or more deep, each man carrying a long pike and a· short sword. When that lot started pounding towards you, look out! Goodbye, limbs, stomach, breath, life! The great advantage of the Phalanx, at least for its general, was that around the perimeter could be placed the professional soldiers, the tough, aggressive men who always love a fight, and in the middle could be placed the farmers, the peasants, the family men, the raggle-taggle and downright weaklings and cowards. Deserters have always been a problem for emperors and generals. There are always too many men in an army who want to be fed, not to fight. But Alexander really cracked the problem. Once the Phalanx began its thunderous charge there was no running away for any of its composite members. If a man so much as hesitated he would be trampled to death. Safer by far to go with it than to flee. And this is the principle to which all Alexander's successors have held – make it kill or be killed, charge or be trampled, slash or be slashed, push the button or be incinerated. Bully for you, Alexander!

There was more to Alexander's army than just the Phalanx, of course. Generals like to embroider and decorate, as much as anyone: not merely to be on the safe side, but because deployment can then become an art; there is justification

for much pacing up and down; all kinds of difficult judgements can be made and important decisions taken. Battles
must be fun, or what's the point of them? Defeats must be
dramatic and victories glorious, or all you are left with is
the trampled, messy mud-and-blood and smelly severed
limbs of the battlefield. So, in front of the Phalanx, before
it started its battering run, would go a skirmish line, made
up of bad servants, inefficient foragers, criminals and so
forth, armed with bows, javelins, darts and slings, who
would harry and tease the enemy, and seldom survived, but
needed a lot of organisation. And wheeling and dealing
around the side of the Phalanx, surrounding and protecting
their Emperor, were the young noblemen, Alexander's elite
corps of cavalry, who could be relied upon to grasp, as the
peasants so often failed to do, such concepts as Valour,
Liberty, Loyalty, Endeavour, and Sacrifice. This particular
cavalry corps set a great example for similar young men
throughout the Age of Muscle, and well into the Age of
Gunpowder. Do you think Alexander's infantry died cheer-
ing him? That we will never know. Those who wrote about
battles in the past liked to assume that this was how soldiers
behaved. I prefer to believe that they come to their
senses as they gasp their last, and the boots of their own
side trample them into the mud, and think 'What am I
doing here? How did I allow this to happen? Is fun for the
others worth this for me?' I may be wrong.

Be that as it may. Panza Jordan and Sergei Wootton, during
the course of Friday afternoon, were put, respectively, in
the rooms where they would be least happy, the former in
Tiglath-Pileser III, where the heating was inadequate, and
the latter in Alexander, which was reputed to be haunted,
for reasons which will later be made clear. They turned up
together on the Academy doorstep as snow began to fall,
and Muffin let them in. Both men blamed Muffin, not Joan
Lumb, for the wretchedness of their rooms, which she
had expected. Employees so often carry the can for their
employers.

44

10

Acorn the butler opened the great front door of the Shrapnel Academy in response to General Leo Makeshift's ring. The General and Bella stepped inside, and a flurry of snow blew in with them. Acorn sent the houseman Raindrop to see to the garaging of the car. Joan Lumb stepped forward to welcome the General and rather half-heartedly greet his young secretary Bella.

Acorn took the opportunity of asking Muffin where exactly the General's chauffeur and the General's secretary were to be put, since Joan Lumb had issued no orders, and now Ivor stood at the back of the hall, waiting, embarrassed, and as it were undesignated.

'She's a little indecisive today,' said Muffin, kindly.

'It's all the excitement, and of course Murray's coming.'

Joan Lumb believed her feelings for Murray were well disguised, but of course they were not. Everyone knew but Murray. 'Besides,' added Muffin, 'she does like to *see* people first. But I'll ask her for a decision.'

At the Shrapnel Academy the grand ground-floor rooms were used for dining, lecturing and relaxing. On the first floor were the suites where visiting dignitaries and lecturers were accommodated – the Queen's sister herself had once stayed in the Charlemagne Suite. On the second floor were the smaller but still pleasant student, cadet and Academy staff bedrooms, and on the attic floor were the small dormered rooms where visiting white servants slept. The Shrapnel servants slept in dormitories in the semi-basement and basement which made up the kitchen and service areas of the great house. And if they slept five to a bed, and six under it, Joan Lumb was not to know. Their children were trained not to cough or cry when she was on her monthly round of dormitory inspection. Old ladies stayed their wheezing and old men their coughing, while Joan Lumb strode by. They pressed themselves into the cupboards and alcoves of this dank, subterranean world, and lived to see another day.

In Joan Lumb's mind the status scale ran thus:

> Employers, male, white
> Employers, female, white
> Servants, male, white
> Employees, male, black
> Servants, female, white
> Employees, female, black
> Servants, male, black
> Servants, female, black

This seemed to Joan the natural order of things; and exceptions, of course, proved the rule. Both Ivor and Bella, on first sight, presented Joan Lumb with difficulties. It was rare for a servant to be as blond as Ivor the chauffeur. His very blondness seemed to qualify him for more than a servant's room; on the other hand he was a chauffeur – fairly low down the servant scale. And what about Bella? A secretary? Surely she, by virtue of her pallor and the carved, still quality of her perfect face, all but qualified for a room on the second floor? Moreover, she was coming to dinner. But no, look again. She was no secretary, she was the General's tart. Her blouse was thin and cheap and she wore a ridiculous gold cross at her neck.
'The third floor for Miss Morthampton, Acorn,' said Joan Lumb. 'And for the chauffeur too, of course.'

All this detail as to where guests are put and why must seem tedious to some, and I hope they will bear with me, but anyone with more than one spare mattress at their disposal will understand the calculations which go on in the hostly mind: will the doubleness of the bed make up for the twanging of its springs? is it the oldest guest or the most entertaining who deserves the quilt which does not lose

46

feathers? who's to get the spare bed in the child's room – the heaviest sleeper or the one least likely to take offence? And he or she will sympathise with the likes of Joan Lumb and see themselves in her, in this small manner, or that. We must lose our good opinion of ourselves if the world is to be changed, and see ourselves in those we most dislike.

I must tell you rather more about Acorn the butler; he was the uncrowned king of the downstairs domain. Acorn Jeffreys was young, shiny black, languid of speech, brilliant of smile, quick of thought. Plucked as an adolescent from his native Soweto, he had been shipped North and educated by a white welfare agency far, far beyond his parents' expectation. Both bad and good fairies danced attendance at Acorn's birth. The bad doomed him to Soweto and an absentee mother – absent against her will, of course; money has to be earned if children are to be fed, but the child takes little notice of maternal motives and sees only maternal conduct – and the good granted him magnificent good looks and a fine intelligence, the wherewithal of his salvation.

Acorn had passed well enough through the white man's schools and university, but had been sent down from his law college, not for revolutionary activity, but more simply, for non-payment of his fees. Acorn had given the money to SWORD (Student World Organisation for Revolution and Democracy), instead, and argued his right to do so. But educational institutions are much the same the world over. They are, on the whole, kindly, but how can they keep going if students will not pay their fees? They will make do somehow if a pupil who can provide no money provides gratitude and comfortable notions, but if a pupil offers nothing pleasant, why put up with him? Can you blame them for expelling him? Now, partly from choice and partly from necessity – for his government would not allow him home – Acorn worked with the needy and oppressed, in the servant quarters of the Shrapnel Academy. Acorn had to eat, so he had to serve. The white races, in his experience, were too cunning to give, except in their own interests, and too dangerous to rob. So now Acorn worked for them, as did so many of his countrymen, as had his mother before him, placing their food in front of them, wiping up after them. Acorn ate well, mind you, better than his mother ever had. For now he was at the heart of Empire, where the good things are, and the crumbs which fall from the tables of power are fat and large.

In fact Acorn ate not just crumbs but whole chickens, appropriated from the upstairs table, at the rate of eight or ten a week. The cooks provided them; a simple enough matter – the young gentlemen upstairs ate well, and chickens passed through the kitchen by the hundred. The downstairs staff did not grudge Acorn his luxuries, or if they did, did not show it. Acorn's warm brown eyes could quite quickly turn cold and cruel. The cooks themselves, along with the rest of the staff, these days made do for meat with flakes of chicken flesh left over from the upstairs table. Mixed up with rice, vegetables, lentils and chillis – which will make the poorest dish exciting – it served them well enough. It had to. It was Acorn's habit to commandeer the money allocated – generously enough – by Joan Lumb for the staff table, and send it off weekly to SWORD. Joan Lumb inspected the kitchens once a week. Acorn saw her round, and Joan Lumb saw nothing wrong, and continued to believe that her staff numbered thirty souls. In fact, several hundreds lived in the warrens below, and the numbers grew all the time: babies were born, spouses shipped in, partners acquired, runaways sheltered, and Joan Lumb knew nothing about it.

It did sometimes occur to Hilda, the lovely, gentle Balinese girl who was Acorn's bedfellow, she with the degree in English Literature, to wonder how much of Joan Lumb's Staff Food Allowance was sent to SWORD and how much went into her lover's pocket, but she said nothing. How could she? Why should she? She was trained to love, admire and appreciate, not to criticise. Acorn had spent a summer training with SWORD in the Lebanon, and knew all too well how to deal with opponents, secretly, quickly and effectively. If you are the lover of a man like that you need to go carefully, tread more softly, not less.

Hilda, of course, had not started life as Hilda, any more than Acorn had started life as Acorn. But Joan Lumb, being a member of the literate races, had no time for names which, however full of phonetic and racial resonance, would give difficulty to typists.

'Acorn,' she said, when first he stood before her – he seemed to glisten with pride and strength – 'We will call you Acorn.' 'That from which mighty oaks grow,' he remarked. 'Very well, Acorn it shall be.'

Joan Lumb, having not required this assent, was a little taken aback to receive it. She hoped the young man would not prove uppity. But his English was excellent, and he was intelligent, and cheerful, and there is nothing worse than being served by people who do not understand a simple order, are debased in their humanity, and unhappy. She wanted, quite actively, to have him on the staff. She employed him in the same spirit as a businessman employs a pretty girl rather than a plain one; and then she made him butler, in that same spirit as the headmaster makes a naughty boy a prefect, hoping it will quieten him down.

11

Joan Lumb, since Acorn was occupied with Bella Morthampton and Ivor, herself showed the General to the Charlemagne Suite. The suite was named after the Emperor-
General who did so much, during his reign from AD 771 to
814, to bring grace and style back to warfare after the fall
of the Roman Empire. Battles had degenerated alarmingly
since the days of Tiglath-Pileser and Alexander and, after
them, the glory that was Greece and the grandeur that was
Rome. Battles were no longer informed by tactics, as they
had been in that ancient world. Now there was nothing but
a disorderly alignment of opposing warriors, all shoving and
pushing, in roughly parallel orders of battle, followed by
dull, uninspired butchery (*sic*. I quote a military historian:
it is their habit to make this kind of distinction, between
inspired death-dealing and uninspired butchery) until one
side or the other fled. There was no leadership; no ingenuity,
sophistication or discipline on the battlefield at all. Perfectly
dreadful, military historians agree! Then, as if in answer to
the challenge of the times, Charlemagne emerged. He it was
who brought ritual back into battle, and discipline, oh,
such discipline! Charlemagne established ranks amongst his
troops and efficient lines of command: he developed the arts
of foraging so that his armies could go farther and yet farther
afield – now they could venture a thousand miles from home
or more. Whole nations might go hungry, there might not
be seed for next year's harvest, but the troops would be fed
and the battle be won! And there were always such lots of
troops. Charlemagne's nobles had to provide them, or lose
their lands. So the peasantry lost its freedom, the feudalising
process was hastened, and a good supply of soldiery insured
for centuries to come. Good on you, Charlemagne! Good on
you, cobber!

The suite of course was charming, and done in rococo style which enchanted the General. In the bedroom, however, was a large double bed hung with heavy tapestries, which he hoped was dust free. He had suffered from asthma in his youth, and although now free of the disease, had an automatic fear and suspicion of dust. He had a terrible vision of Bella bouncing naked on the bed, and with each bounce a cloud of dust arising, and himself wheezing and huffing. He need not have worried: the bed was well aired and the hangings and blankets properly shaken, but adulterers make over-anxious, guilty lovers, quite ridiculously nervous of possible catastrophe. And although the General was not consciously guilty, knowing quite well that all through history the brave have deserved the fair, and by definition a general is a brave man, he was, all the same, married. 'I'm sure I'll be most comfortable here,' said the General, bravely. 'A really enchanting room! And what an interesting bed.'

'A bed with a history,' said Joan Lumb. 'It's called the Charlemagne bed. The Queen's sister once slept in it.' These things do not go forgotten.

12

Now, gentle reader, shall we return to the Blades, whom we last saw sailing in their Volvo past the unfortunate Mew from the *Woman's Times*.

Gentle reader! What have I said! You are no more gentle than I am. I apologise for insulting you. You are as ferocious as anyone else. The notion that the reader is gentle is very bad for both readers and writers – and the latter do tend to encourage the former in this belief. We all believe ourselves to be, more or less, well intentioned, nice – goodies in fact, whether we're the greengrocer or the Shah of Shahs. But we can't possibly be, or how would the world have got into the state it's in? Who else but ourselves are doing this to ourselves? We simply don't know our own natures.

Consider Shirley. Driving along with Victor sleeping beside her, and Serena, Piers and Nell all agreeably crumpled up in the back seat, and Harry trembling and travelling behind the mesh. Shirley seems gentle and ordinary and perfectly pleasant – of all the people in this book so far by far the nicest. She certainly believes herself to be amiable enough. But she wouldn't stop to give Mew a lift, would she? No! Don't you think a perfect person would have, a truly good, unselfish woman? The kind we all appreciate, ought to want to be? Shirley knew Mew was in danger from the weather, and from possible rape at the hands of the likes of Baf, and still she left her standing there at the side of the road. What sort of sisterhood is that? Baf was about to come along. Had Baf been less civilised, less chivalrous, he might well have cried outrage at Mew's refusal to be helped, and used his hurt feelings as an excuse for sexual aggression; and do not forget, Baf was armed, wonderfully armed, albeit in miniature, with his hand-weapons (none bigger than a lady's cigarette-lighter) with their bullets like those silver balls you put on birthday cakes, which enlarge and engorge and explode so violently when meeting human flesh. And how could Mew have resisted had he chosen to threaten her with this power? Baf did not choose, he would not so choose, but how exciting that power is. *He could have chosen.* Sex, death, megadeath: if one, why not a million, or a million million? Shrapnel to the power of five hundred thousand in a knife box at the back of a car! Oh, Henry Shrapnel, if you knew what you were doing, or what path you were on, when you invented the exploding cannonball, would you have hesitated? I think not. Who can be responsible, here and now, for what the future does? Are *we*?

Plaintive civilian whines! How Joan Lumb sneers at them!

Joan Lumb had not been unprepared for her small visitors. They trailed sleepily into the Shrapnel Academy after their parents, a doll in Serena's hand, a woolly lamb in Nell's, and a teddy in Piers'. Shirley thought they looked perfectly sweet.
'I knew you'd bring the children,' said Joan Lumb, looking at them with distaste. She had already asked Hilda to prepare the nursery, Genghis Khan on the first floor, albeit at the back of the house.

'Say hello to your Auntie,' said Victor to Serena, Piers and Nell, and thank God they did, rubbing sleepy eyes, awed by the expanse of polished parquet, dark brown panelling, lofty ceiling, portraits of generals and occasionally their wives, who gazed down upon them, stern but kind. Shirley would never have suggested they so greet their aunt, knowing that refusal could only offend. But it was, after all, in Victor's nature to take risks, and succeed. That was why, she assumed, he had risen so far at Gloabal.
'Hello, Auntie,' said Serena.
'Hello, Auntie,' said Piers.
'Allo Wanty,' said Nell.

'She doesn't speak very well,' said Joan Lumb. 'Is she all right?'

'That's how three-year-olds speak,' said Shirley, firmly.

Joan Lumb raised her eyebrows.

'We didn't mean to bring them,' said Shirley, 'but we had to because the girl gave notice.'

'It's always hopeless employing Europeans,' said Joan Lumb. 'They imagine they're as good as you are, and are hopelessly overpaid, which unsettles them. But you would have found some other reason for bringing them, Shirley. I know you would.'

'They're only little for such a short time,' said Shirley, helplessly. She was right. The world whirls on, season gives way to season, and before you know it, the child is the grown man, the grown woman.

'For quite long enough,' said Joan Lumb. She had never wanted children. Procreation, it seemed to her, was altogether too chancy a business. There was no controlling a child's genes, and there were, in her experience, a number of traits which no amount of early training seemed able to eradicate. She had herself been fortunate enough to escape weak-mindedness. Victor, on the other hand, had inherited a sentimental streak, which had made it impossible for him to join the army. He could wield the power of life and death but only from a distance, by means of shuffling pieces of paper about. He did not have the guts, as Joan had once remarked to the Colonel, to deal with the Ace of Spades.

Joan Lumb clapped her hands. Hilda appeared, her curved and sensuous mouth gently smiling.

'Hilda,' said Joan Lumb, 'take the children to Genghis Khan. Bath them, feed them, put them to bed.'

'Yes, madam,' lisped Hilda, and the children followed where she led, up the stairs and down corridors, such was the authority in Joan Lumb's voice, the enticement in Hilda's walk, without so much as looking back. Or perhaps it was that the portraits frightened them? You know what portraits are – how the eyes seem to follow the guilty. And who guiltier than small children, who know well enough the trouble and torment to which they put the adult world? No wonder they're frightened of the dark. No wonder they have nightmares. It is their own selves terrify them.

Serena went first, mousey and round-faced and prim; then Piers, sombre and brooding; then Nell, blonde, wide-eyed and giggly. Charming! And Hilda glided in front of them, demure, her look liquid, her limbs graceful: these being the rewards of gratified desire, and Acorn much given and very able so to gratify her. Hilda had made one of the broom cupboards beneath the servants' stairs into a place where he and she could love in privacy and grace: she had hung it with rich fabrics from the linen cupboard, and floored and lined it with feather quilts and cushions and hung amulets here and there: such a place, such a shrine to sensual needs, was invaluable to both of them, since below stairs the male and female staff slept in segregated dormitories. Acorn had recently commandeered an entire dormitory to himself, the better to hold staff meetings. Those thus displaced in the community interest doubled up elsewhere and did well enough, or simply slept on the floor, if that was what they were accustomed to. But Acorn preferred to meet Hilda under the stairs, in the broom cupboard, and no doubt had his reasons. And it was, as we have seen, Hilda's part to accept, not question. The broom cupboard, incidentally, was adjacent to the Alexander Room, and it was the unexplained noises which so often arose from the cupboard which had given rise to the rumour that the room was haunted.

Shirley's eyes followed the children, as they went with Hilda. She was anxious. They were going with a stranger, and so quietly! But how could she demur? Joan's manner denied it. So, when it came to it, did her husband's. Victor believed in mother-love, of course; and, as do all civilised people, that the child is happiest in the mother's company – though the mother not always in the child's. But at the moment Victor believed in delegation even more than mother-love. Self-interest defeated paternal concern. The children would be safe enough: he wanted peace, and relaxation, and his wife's company while he changed for dinner. And she wanted, for herself, the same thing of him. Of course. These are the rewards of married life, and why should we not have them?

Honestly, friends, we have to take shifts at virtue. We can't keep it up all the time, relentlessly, not even mother-love, least of all sexual loyalty. Look how a decade's fidelity can flash within the drunken, silvery hour into infidelity – does that devalue all that went before?

Yes, is the answer. Yes, yes, yes. Where shall we find the saint amongst us?

Oddly, Joan Lumb thinks she has found the saint, the Hero, in Henry Shrapnel. In her mind he is second only to Murray. She would have him sanctified if she could. She plans to make a speech about Henry Shrapnel and his contribution to military history – which is *all* history in her view – when she replies to the toast 'The Shrapnel Academy' at the Eve-of-Waterloo dinner.

Be all that as it may, off went the children to Genghis Khan. The suite had a rather unfortunate view over the waste-disposal area. Not, of course, that this mattered for the moment, since it was dark, and beginning to snow quite hard besides, and the snow would soon obliterate ugliness and make everything, even dustbins, pure and beautiful. The room was kept especially for children: it contained four small beds, two cots, an adjacent cubicle for a resident babysitter, and a small kitchenette where food could be prepared, and children, presumably, kept self-contained.

Genghis Khan, the Whirlwind from Mongolia, working and striving around and about the year 1200, was another who did a wonderful job, unifying his people and turning them into an all but invincible military organisation. Genghis Khan's horse troops swarmed all over Asia, plundering, killing, devastating, learning as they went new tricks of defence and attack; and the arts of siegecraft – how to use siege engines, mangonels, giant catapults: how to dig tunnels under the fortifications of besieged cities, and enter by stealth – how best to shower flames upon those within, and enter under cover of smoke-screen, how to herd captives before them so defenders were forced to kill their own kind. Genghis Khan went south, north and east, slaughtering, laying waste, burning, wonderfully successful – and why? Because he had one of the best-organised and most thoroughly disciplined armies ever created. It was quality, not quantity, that counted: those Mongol hordes were scarcely hordes; rather they were crack teams. All were on horseback. Forty per cent were heavy cavalry, for shock action: each man completely armoured and carrying a lance, with a scimitar in his belt. And behind would come the 60 per cent of light cavalry, without armour, but with bows and scimitars, whose function was reconnaissance, screening, the provision of firepower support to the 40 per cent and general mopping-up operations. Each man wore a vest of raw, tightly woven silk so that if he got hit by an enemy arrow surgeons could extract the arrowhead by pulling out the silk. And the horses! They were wonderful. They could live off the land, go for days without food, and in general sustain themselves. And because they were mostly mares, the men could live off their milk, and did, and occasionally carve a slice of meat off a livng rump. Brilliant! Genghis Khan's intelligence network was superb – it spread throughout Europe and Asia, spies travelling in the disguise of merchants or traders. The Mongols used every trick and ruse they could: they had no notion of chivalry: of armies waiting for a signal to advance. All they wanted was to kill and not be killed: they were not interested in honour or renown; they were in love with their own cunning. They would move fastest in the hard winter when the marshes were frozen and rivers ice and everyone else stayed home. (They would find out just how safe the ice was by driving local populations out upon it. Whoops! Sorry! Oh, the joke of it!) They loved to burn crops and prairies and towns simply to hide their movements. They loved to declare peace and then slaughter the vanquished when they least expected it. It was fun, fun, fun! And then the Mongols turned west and Europe shivered but somehow they had outgrown their strength. They slipped off away home, for no reason anyone can quite grasp. That's the way things go. Empires rise and fall. Perhaps death's appetite is cyclical. Perhaps she gets indigestion. Perhaps even her gorge rises with so much blood.

13

Joan Lumb proudly showed her brother around the Shrapnel Academy. It was warm inside, almost uncomfortably so; it was possible to ignore completely the north wind rising on the other side of the thick stone walls. Corridors were well carpeted, walls well insulated; lights illuminated dark corners, and spotlights shone from strips upon paintings by artists of note, even in the remoter parts of the building. She showed him the library, second in pride only to that of London's Imperial War Museum, where every battle, every campaign, every victory, every defeat of recorded history was described and depicted with that mixture of awe and horror and excitement which moves even the most sober of military historians.

'A favourite room with our students,' she said. 'The more sensible of them realise that wide background reading is the key to good exam results. We have Sergei Wootton – you know Sergei, the art historian? He had his own arts programme on the television not so long ago. I didn't watch it myself but those who did said it was excellent.'

Victor said he hadn't heard of Sergei Wootton but looked forward to meeting him. Shirley said she'd seen the programme but Joan Lumb took no notice, only looked as if she wondered why Shirley was tagging along.

She took Victor to the Games Room which, besides the pool table, the dartboard, and so on, had its own little shooting gallery, where cardboard cutouts of the Russian Premier travelled along at the back of the range, and must be hit in the head if points were to be scored.

'Such fun!' said Joan Lumb and Shirley shuddered rather pointedly, and loudly. Victor frowned at her slightly.

'Sorry!' she whispered. 'Couldn't help it!'

'She is my sister!' he reproached her, as Joan went to retrieve two stray ping-pong balls, un-swept up by a careless staff.

'The servants are terrible,' Joan announced. 'They are absolutely incapable of using their own initiative. And one simply can't think of everything oneself.'

So her mother had spoken: so no doubt her daughter would, did she have one. Perhaps it was fortunate she did not. She took Victor to the lecture rooms, and the dining halls, and the press office, and he pretended to be interested, out of kindness. She wanted him to be proud of her. She said that the heating bills were phenomenal and the electricity bills astronomical: power lines had to travel over hill and dale to reach the Academy, and were vulnerable to weather, so she had an emergency back-up system installed. It was fortunate the Academy was so well funded. At least she did not have to scrub around for money, as she understood so many other institutions did.

'People realise the importance of defence,' she said. 'And the importance of ideas in the war against communism. The army, the government, and insurers are all generous. We are particularly fortunate in bequests.'

'I see you love the job,' said Victor.

'Sometimes,' said his sister, 'I'm almost glad the Colonel died. I would never have thought of taking up this post if I had not been a widow. A wife's first duty must always be to her husband. He must have first call on her time and attention.'

'What about the children?' asked Shirley. 'Shouldn't they come first?'

'Shirley,' said Joan Lumb, 'if you want to go to your room, Muffin will show you the way.'

But when she went looking for Muffin, Joan Lumb found that she was not available. Baf had arrived and Muffin was showing him to his room.

'That can't take for ever,' said Joan Lumb crossly, but the look on Acorn's face suggested that it might take some considerable time. Joan Lumb sighed, but could not give the matter her proper attention because Acorn told her that Murray Fairchild had arrived and was waiting in the blue living-room. Joan went at once. She was wearing a new silk dress in reds and oranges which she knew suited her; they were Murray's favourite colours. He had once told her so. When he was a child, he said, his blanket was in red and orange, and he had often hidden beneath it to avoid trouble. Now he associated the colours with safety, warmth, sleep.

Joan Lumb had allocated the Gustavus Adolphus Suite to Murray Fairchild. These were her favourite rooms. The furniture was heavy oak and very old; the walls were panelled. The bed was big and soft; in the bathroom a heavy white bath stood proudly on little Victorian feet, and water gushed from a wide faucet. The television set was cunningly hidden in a mahogany commode. The words 'Gustavus Adolphus' were embossed in gold above the door.

Reader, you now fear you are going to hear all about Gustavus Adolphus. How right you are! Gustavus Adolphus assumed the Swedish throne in 1611. Adolphus was one of the Military Greats: tactician, strategist, administrator, leader of men, educated in the military arts from an early age, knowing everything the human race had so far worked out about gunnery, horsemanship, siegecraft, employment of fortifications, drill and logistics. What he didn't have was an army, or a war. Gustavus introduced national conscription, hired mercenaries, and one way and another invented the modern army. He formed artillery regiments, cavalry squadrons, and got rid of cumbersome, heavy guns. He invented the sturdy 3-pounder, the regimental gun, with packaged cartridge and simplified loading, which gave such a good rate of fire. By 1631 he had a state army, 30,000 strong: an army strict and democratic, no longer confined to the nobility and the peasants, but now drawing in the middle classes too. The wars came thick and fast. (If you own a new nut-cracker, you pretty soon have nuts to crack.) His influence on European warfare was profound. The casualty rate remained high, at 30 per cent for those he defeated and 20 per cent of his own victorious troops blown up, slashed, or trampled by the hooves or artillery of both sides, but it was with Gustavus Adolphus that the Age of Gunpowder really got under way. He was one of the Men of History whom Joan Lumb most admired, and she knew that Murray would be happy in the room.

If we are to get the better of Joan Lumb, we must know more than she does: that is why we have had these boring lectures on Tiglath-Pileser, Adolphus, Augustus, and so forth. We must also know more about ourselves, which is on the whole more entertaining, and that is why Bella Morthampton, Leo Makeshift, Ivor the chauffeur, Victor and Shirley Blade and the little Blades, Baf Winchester, Murray Fairchild, Panza Jordan, Sergei Wootton, Muffin Aldred and Joan Lumb are all gathered together under the sound and well-funded roof of the Shrapnel Academy. For what is the point of fiction except self-discovery?

14

Snow fell, spreading from the western regions, at first gently, heavy flake by heavy flake; then, as the wind rose, in smaller, tougher, flying gobbets. Downstairs the servants debated, severally in their many languages, then jointly, in English the master tongue, whether or not to fight the stuff from the door with spades, shovels and brooms. The night might well bring a thaw; and even if it did not and the snow continued, all effort must in the end be wasted. Snow was like that, as those who had spent more than a winter in this foreign climate could attest. Time disposed of it more effectively than man. Snow fell, and froze, and hampered normal activity to one degree or another, but then at least it disappeared, leaving everything much as it had been before. It was preferable, any day, to earthquake, volcano, tidal flood or cyclone, all of which had the power to alter the landscape itself.

Upstairs, Joan Lumb was listening too intently to Murray's words, waiting too hopefully for Murray's smile, to pay much attention to the blizzard outside. Rendered soft and impractical by desire, she quite forgot to organise. Snow whistled through the air and grew thicker and yet thicker on the ground, and Joan Lumb did nothing. She complained a little about the lateness of the journalist from *The Times*, and decided to delay dinner on her account for half an hour, no more, and deplored her rudeness in not at least telephoning to explain herself.

(Sisters, this is no criticism of the female state, that love should thus make a strong woman impractical. Men are no different. They lose whole empires in a loved one's eyes, lose God himself, and think nothing of it. Pity Caesar's Antony, pity Sampson, pity poor Joan Lumb.)

'It may be the weather,' said Murray. He had once spent a winter on the Falkland Islands, trapping a saboteur who was falsifying reports on mineral deposits to the south. He'd been tricked and tripped and lamed and almost frozen to death. He knew cold lands as well as hot.

'Oh, poof, Murray!' said Joan. 'A little snow! People make far too much fuss!' She had snowballed and sledged as a child, and blown warm breath on chilly hands, and loved every minute of it. Snow had never stopped Joan Lumb doing anything she wanted.

Murray had declined whisky, saying it gave him indigestion, and coffee, on the grounds that it made his heart race. He asked for Perrier water. Joan Lumb rang for Acorn. This precious hour, alone with Murray! Her heart was light. She was happy enough that dinner was delayed. The other guests had so far kept tactfully to their rooms, waiting for the dinner gong.

The Friday afternoon, below stairs, had not been tranquil. As well as the preparation of cucumber sandwiches and gâteau-au-rhum, it had seen a death, and a tragic one, and witnessed a sudden and unexpected power struggle between Acorn and Inverness, the groundsman, his second-in-command. Inverness, a small, quiet, grey, bespectacled ear surgeon from Pakistan, who enjoyed the trust and confidence of the downstairs community, had challenged Acorn's authority.

This is what happened.

Miriam, a young woman from Sri Lanka, of whom both Acorn and Inverness were fond, was in labour in one of the back pantries, a small but warm and well-lit room frequently used as a hospital. She was attended by Inverness. Inverness had witnessed Bhutto's death in prison: now he hid from

64

Colonel Zia, and no nation would officially have him. So he swept leaves and saved roses from black-spot at the Shrapnel Academy. Those of you who have skills and professions, and can practise them in peace, be grateful. It is not given to everyone so to do.

Miriam was warm and cheerful: her eyes were large and liquid and her mouth soft and sweet. She was not so pretty as Hilda, or so intelligent, but she was worthy of Acorn's attention. The baby which now attempted to batter its way out of her helpless, gentle embrace was his.

'She will have to go to hospital,' said Inverness. 'She has to have a Caesarian.'

'You must do it yourself,' said Acorn. There were no proper facilities for surgery in the pantry, although Inverness had once, triumphantly, there performed a successful appendectomy, using a kitchen knife. It was not possible to involve the health authorities, even in emergencies. Names, passports, visas would be required and none were available. Immigration officers would arrive on the doorstep and deportation for all be the almost inevitable conclusion. The young and vigorous would survive well enough, but the old, the weak, the feeble in mind and body, women and children, the homeless and stateless, would have little future outside the shelter of the Shrapnel Academy.

'There is no way I can do it,' said Inverness. 'She will die.'

'She must take her chances,' said Acorn. 'But save the baby, if you can.' Given a choice between mother and baby, the surgeon must save the baby: this is the tradition of the world, and who is to say it is wrong?

So now Miriam sweated and groaned and the baby butted and fought and found no way out. Miriam bled and the flow would not stop. Matilda the Mexican girl used towel after towel sopping up the blood. Drops fell right through the mattress, through the spaces of the rusty wire bed springs and onto the well-swept, well-scoured floor. The bright bare lightbulb flickered and dimmed, as the wind and snow hit the power lines, but then recovered. Inverness

65

used his kitchen knife, and saved the baby. Otherwise both would have died. Inverness rocked the baby to his slight chest, and wept, and presently went with the child in his arms to the staff dining-room. Acorn sat at the head of the table, devouring a chicken, tearing it to pieces with strong, greasy hands. All around him stood and sat the staff, half-admiring, half-alarmed, more civilised by half than he, but twice as helpless.

'Acorn,' said Inverness.

'Lord Acorn—' said Acorn.

'You're joking,' said Inverness.

'I am not,' said Acorn, and the people around grew still.

'Lord Acorn,' said Inverness, 'here is your baby. Miriam is dead.' A sigh went up: a sob or so, quickly silenced. 'Something like this was bound to happen sooner or later. We can't go on this way.'

Acorn put down his chicken. He looked at his own strong powerful hands. They were good for tearing meat, for strangling. They could also make love wonderfully, for all the good that that had done Miriam. He did not speak at once.

'Miriam's blood is not on my hands,' he said. His voice began to rise. 'Guilt rests with those upstairs, who have deprived us of our freedom. The scales must be righted. There must be justice! We will have vengeance!'

He shouted the last word, releasing his audience from their burden of quiet: those who spoke English translated the words for the benefit of those who did not: there was an agreeable and exciting buzz of voice and communion.

'Mad,' thought Inverness. 'Finally flipped. What have I done? Triggered a psychotic response? I should have kept my mouth shut.'

'Vengeance,' said Inverness to the crowd, 'is not an appropriate response,' but he didn't have the trick of public speaking, and very few took any notice. Why should they? Acorn had charisma: Inverness had not. Acorn said what they wanted to hear: what Inverness said was boring. Inverness handed the baby to Matilda for safekeeping, and prudently left the room, before Acorn's anger could focus on the bringer of bad news. A few like-minded allies went with him.

That was during the Friday afternoon. By the time the guests arrived, and the gâteau-au-rhum was prepared, the servants' quarters were throbbing with the pleasure-pain of welling subversive thought, as a boil throbs excitingly, just before it bursts. Acorn came striding down the vaulted corridor to the blue living-room where Joan Lumb spent this precious hour alone with Murray Fairfield. He opened the door without knocking, as he was right to do – a good butler only ever knocks on the doors of bedrooms – and stood framed in the doorway, shiny black, energetic. Murray sat peacefully on one side of the wide fireplace, and the leaping flames sent shadows over his grizzled face. Joan Lumb sat on the other side; she turned her flushed face slowly towards Acorn: she looked almost pretty, almost young, almost soft. So much love does. Murray, of course, thought she looked like this all the time. How could he not?
'Acorn,' she said. 'Did I ring? Yes, I rang. Some Perrier water for Mr Fairfield.'
'Madam,' said Acorn, 'on your instructions we keep no Perrier water in the house.' And this was true enough. Joan Lumb objected strongly to paying through the nose for water, however charmingly bottled, however lively to the palate, for did not water fall freely from the sky, and run freely through the fields, and flow all but freely from taps? But now Murray asked for Perrier water, and she had none!
'Well then, Acorn,' she said. 'Bring Mr Fairfield some iced water and lemon.'
'No lemon,' said Murray. 'Too acid for my digestion. I'm happiest these days on just plain mealie-bud mash.' Whatever that might be.
'Iced water, Acorn,' said Joan.
'Hold the ice, Acorn,' said Murray. 'Too much of a shock to the system. Room temperature. Tap water will do me

fine.' Acorn bowed politely, and went to do Joan Lumb's bidding. As for Murray, he concluded that Joan Lumb was a good sort of woman, as white women went, and politeness was due to her as his hostess, but she did fuss, and not as brown women fussed, with soft looks and touches and smiles, but awkwardly, as if a dog, attempting to be a cat, had jumped on a lap. Murray imagined there were little brown women amongst the staff – he had seen the flash of a young dusky shoulder vanishing down a corridor when he arrived, the movement of small buttocks under silk – and hoped Joan Lumb would have the sense to see that one came knocking at his door during the night. But he doubted it. That was the trouble with having women in men's jobs.

'Plain water and mealie-buds,' cried Joan Lumb. 'A man who risks not just his life but his digestion in the cause of freedom – oh, Murray!'

She laid her hand on his. It seemed to Murray a curious thing, very large and white, and the nails were blood-red. But he did not like to remove it. He even felt some explanation was necessary.

'I was once made to drink acid in a San Salvadorian jail,' he said. 'My insides haven't been the same since. Fortunately I was able to get to water in time. They were doing the drowning trick. They hold your head under water, let you up, hold you under – well, I just swallowed and neutralised the acid. Torturers are stupid people. It's the only hope one has.'

'Oh, Murray!' The hand tightened. He patted it.

'Actually I didn't hold my tongue that time,' said Murray. 'I talked. Broke.'

Why was he telling her this? This plain white woman whom nobody loved?

'But that's true courage, isn't it,' she said, and he was grateful. 'Not just heroics. To know fear, succumb to it, recover, carry on –'

'It made no difference, of course. The people I betrayed had already been discovered, wiped out –'

'Not betrayal, don't say betrayed –'

68

'But it was betrayal,' he said, sadly. 'Once I broke, they simply let me go. I guess they were disappointed in me. I'd let everyone down: friends, foes, myself. I can't tell you what I felt. It was worse than pain.'

He found he was weeping: his hand clenched upon hers: hers responded. In all the rest of my life, she thought, they can't take this moment away from me. It is happening, it has happened. Murray Fairchild holds Joan Lumb's hand, trusts her, and weeps.

'I'm sorry,' he said presently. 'I guess it's just that you remind me of my mother.'

Her heart seemed to falter. It was a shock. It was not at all what she had hoped to hear. How cruel life is, to women of a certain age, who keep forgetting that that is what they are.

At that moment Acorn returned with a glass of water.

'Thank you, Acorn,' she said. And then – 'Acorn, you touched the rim of the glass with your hand. Go downstairs and fetch another. I know you people have no grasp of hygiene, but couldn't you at least try to learn?'

Well, she was upset. Acorn didn't hit her or kill her, he just went to fetch another glass. He was biding his time.

15

'Shall I just pop in and look at the children?' asked Shirley of Victor. She had changed into a flowered linen dress. She looked clean and decorous, pretty but not glamorous. She had three children under seven. She had shelved all that other for the time being. One day, one day!

'You'd only disturb them,' said Victor.

'I expect you're right,' said Shirley. She wanted a drink; not badly, but enough to be conscious of it. She tried not to drink, and mostly managed not to. She did not want to be like her sister, Valerie. Shirley had opened a closet in Valerie's house, mistaking it for the bathroom door, and empty gin bottles had tumbled out. Some had broken. It had been embarrassing. Valerie said she was saving them to make indoor tropical gardens to give to people at Christmas, but the explanation was not convincing.

'Shall we go downstairs?' she asked Victor. She thought he looked particularly handsome, and said so. He put his arms round her and gave her cheek a little peck.

'I have a funny feeling,' said Shirley, 'that something not very nice is going to happen.'

'We might be snowed in,' said Victor, peering out of the tall windows. 'That might not be very nice.'

'I bought snow chains,' said Shirley, virtuously. 'You know there was a hitchhiker on the road? I nearly stopped.'

'But you didn't stop,' he said.

'I feel bad about it,' she said. 'Perhaps she'd run out of petrol, perhaps she was a genuine case.'

'Perhaps she was part of an organisation which kidnaps senior executives and holds them to ransom,' he said. He was part-joking, part not. Such things happened. He had put on a dark grey suit, silky to the feel. His socks were dark red.

'Hardly after dark on a country road,' she said.

'Mostly after dark on a country road,' he said.

'Anyway,' said Shirley, 'the children were asleep. She'd have woken them up getting in.'

'Quite so. First, we must look after our own: after that, if there's a surplus, we can look after other people. Our children must sleep, and she risk rape. That's the way it goes. Besides, when they're awake they're very noisy children. It's safer for you to drive while they sleep.'

'I think I should have stopped, all the same,' said Shirley. 'It was somehow an unlucky thing of me to have done, not to have stopped.'

'Not-stopping is not doing something,' said Victor, 'it is merely failing to do something.'

'All the same!' said Shirley, and shivered.

Victor and Shirley went downstairs to join Joan and Murray, locking the door behind them, though this was not customary in the Shrapnel Academy, where a high standard of honesty normally prevailed. But those who steal are always anxious about being stolen from: and Victor was the thief of other men's life and labour, as it is almost impossible for men in industry not to be.

Now. Your appetite for facts has perhaps returned? Your documentary indigestion has abated? You are ready for Napoleon, the greatest military genius of all time? (Joan Lumb places Henry Shrapnel above him but that is surely just perversity. Shrapnel was an inventor, a scientist, not a leader of men. Joan Lumb would argue that a leader is nothing without weapons, which is true enough, but what are weapons if there is nobody to organise their deployment?) During the Middle Ages there had been yet another decline in battle management. Charlemagne and Gustavus Adolphus were forgotten. Armies now simply met head on in pitched battles: Agincourt, Cressy, Sedgemoor, and so forth. Opposing forces, some mounted, some on foot, would sway this way and that over a confined patch of ground (armies 100,000 strong would be deployed against one

71

another in areas of only a few square kilometres) slashing and hacking over terrain which became increasingly difficult as the dead and dying piled up underfoot. Death was for the most part by trampling, crushing and asphyxiation. Who actually won was hard to determine. Napoleon found this battle-system barbaric. A great general needs to exercise great skill. He changed the face of warfare once again. He went to battle with flair, style and skill. Casualty rates fell sharply during the Napoleonic wars, as compared to early wars. The average casualty rate in 1600 was 30 per cent for the defeated and 20 per cent for the victors. By 1820 it had fallen to 23 per cent for the defeated and 19 per cent for the victors. (That is if you leave out the French adventure in Russia in 1812, when the death rate was 80 per cent for the defeated and 90 per cent for the victors, but that was an exception, and it is unfair to count that in the statistics – in the same way that it is unhelpful to average out a child's exam results, when the child gets 90 per cent for English and 10 per cent for Maths. What you do not have here is an average child!) Napoleon did not wish to win at any cost, but to keep that cost down as far as possible and still achieve a victory. Therein, according to Napoleon and his successors, lies the skill, charm and achievement of warfare. The quest is for bigger, better weapons, inflicting maximum casualties on the enemy, but minimum damage to your own troops. (The casualty rate for civilians goes for the most part uncatalogued by army historians. They do not find it interesting.) Even so, at the Battle of Waterloo, in 1815, horses still slipped in the blood and dismounted their riders, so that important messages never got through.

This failure in communications was one of the factors which led to Napoleon's defeat at Waterloo, and his successors (generals learn by their defeat) have been perfecting codes and communication devices ever since. The other factor was the sheer weight of man and gun power which opposed him. The relative combat power of the attacker (Wellington and the allies) against the defender (Napoleon) was 1:·79. Heavy odds against Napoleon! On the other hand, French combat effectiveness (that is to say, the efficiency with which Napoleon deployed men and weapons) was far greater than that of the English: to the ratio of 1:·61. The French had superiority in leadership, training, experience and what the military are pleased to call 'intangible variables'. Nevertheless, they lost the battle; too few men by far faced too many, and communications failed. Generals ever since have done their best when in a conflict situation to avoid these two eventualities. In the First World War, between England and Germany, thousands upon thousands upon thousands upon thousands upon thousands of men were poured in by either side, in the attempt to outnumber the other: and how the Morse coders clicked and semaphores gleamed so there was no danger to the lines of command by messengers slipping in blood and mud. The French, by the way, claim victory at Waterloo. They inflicted more casualties on the allies than the allies did on them. Victory and defeat is a matter of interpretation, and what happens next.

At the Shrapnel Academy there was a whole Napoleon wing, but most of it was closed for redecoration during the Wellington Weekend. Victor and Shirley were in the only part of it which remained open; and there was a strong smell of paint in the rooms, particularly in the bathroom. They were glad to close the door behind them.

16

Meanwhile, in the Gustavus Adolphus Suite, the General rehearsed the next day's speech with Bella as his audience. The General wore a navy velvet suit which showed off his high complexion and thick white hair to advantage: Bella wore a simple black dress. Both of them admired themselves in mirrors from time to time, when they thought the other wasn't looking. The General's wife did not like him wearing velvet: it made her uneasy. Bella's mother had once urged her never to wear black, saying it did nothing for her complexion. She had worn it a great deal ever since: it was not complexion so much as je-ne-sais-quoi which attracted men, but how was Bella's mother to know a thing like that? Bella's mother was a nun and forty-seven when Bella was born, and so far as Bella's mother was concerned, she was virgo intacta and a bride of Christ. There was talk of either miracle, or parthenogenesis, that is to say, self-fertilisation. It happens in snails, of course, and in some of the higher mammals too: eggs begin to divide without fertilisation, growth starts: the child's genes are identical to the mother's: a girl child is born, twin to the mother but a few decades late. And Bella bore an uncanny resemblance to her mother. The Church decided on parthenogenesis, rather than miracle. Had either woman, the mother or the daughter, been rather more likeable, they might well have opted for the latter. Some key in Bella's makeup was flipped during her childhood; which had remained untouched, or thrown the other way, in her mother, and Bella dedicated herself to random fornication in the same spirit as her mother had dedicated herself to Christ: in a kind of all-or-nothing way. 'If you practise too much now,' said Bella, who longed for a drink, and assumed there'd be one downstairs, 'you'll lose the freshness.'

He conceded the point and they went downstairs, meeting Muffin and Baf on the way. Bella was pale and composed, Muffin flushed and fluffy and rumpled, in spite of having brushed out her hair after leaving Baf's bed. Her fringe badly needed cutting. Every hair on Bella's head had, as it were, been individually attended to. Her mother had kept her head shaven under its cowl: some things simply could not go on as they had done in the past.

Baf looked at Bella with interest, as Bella went ahead down the stairs. She wore thin spiky heels and had to go carefully. Muffin, noticing, was upset and puzzled. How could Baf be interested in a woman who looked thin, spiteful and bad tempered? Didn't men like nice, warm, rounded, friendly women, who were careful with and responsive to their feelings? Her mother had told her they did. Muffin, unlike Bella, believed her mother must surely know best: or at any rate had, until this very moment. It occurred to Muffin now, as she came down the stairs, that just as the palate has an appetite for sour as well as sweet, so does the male fancy. Perhaps she should practise being just plain horrid, and see what happened.

17

Now where, you may ask, *is* Mew? You may even be
beginning to feel hungry, as dinner is further and further
delayed. Certainly the guests are. What had held Mew up
between the bottom of the steps where Edna the taxi driver
left her all those pages ago, and the front door? Not the snow:
Mew wore stout flat boots with the laces double-knotted and
could cope with the white stuff easily enough. But visibility
being bad, and her acquaintance with the houses of the
great small, Mew went looking round the back of the house
for what seemed more like a door than the great impassive
oak slab which faced her at the top of the steps. She thought
the slab must serve some decorative rather than functional
purpose and, as the snow on her eyelids obscured her vision
and made the light from the massed carriage lamps flicker
and change, she quite missed the discreet gold bell inset in
the marble columns which flanked the door.

No money had been spared on the Shrapnel Academy over
the years. The army lives well, and knows how to spend,
and likes its buildings at home to be substantial: the better,
no doubt, to withstand the minor blows and explosions of
civil insurrection. When on the move, of course, it is adept
at laying down its giant futon at night and rolling it up in the
morning and moving on, leaving crushed meadow flowers
behind. But look, what's a flower? What's a whole host of
flowers? What are these little passing things, compared to
Glory, Victory, Conquest, Triumph, Freedom and so forth?
Flowers, like people, spring up, open wide, drink in the sun
and rain, fling around a seed or so, fade and die. The living
thing is nothing, the concept all. Why else, but knowing
this, century after century, do generals so cunningly command and soldiers so gladly die? Why else are the giant

cannons of contemporary Europe stocked with neutron bombs which kill life, but leave the structure of civilisation intact? The people will not survive, but the concepts will. This is not madness, as some think, this is sanity indeed. Ask Joan Lumb.

Back to Mew and her stumbling journey round the Shrapnel Academy, searching for entry! Mew's eyes were all but blinded by flying snow, her nose was pink and numb, her cheeks painful in the wind. Her body was warm enough – she wore a Marks & Spencer thermal vest beneath her navy sweater: it was warm, bright red, and prettily lacy. Though Mew affected a tough woman's-wear exterior – it does not do to be too frivolously fancy if you want to keep a job on the *Woman's Times* – she liked to be Hollywood-like next to her skin. That is to say, on the whole silky and sensuous, and if thermal, why then lacy. She even wore oyster satin knickers beneath her jeans. She hoped, as she stumbled, that the Wellington Lecture would be worth her pains, and her expected story on the mad male military ethos up to scratch. She had been surprised at how quickly her request to attend the General's lecture had been granted: more surprised still when the invitation to dinner came. Perhaps the Shrapnel Academy had nothing to hide? She did not want to think so: the general feeling on the *Woman's Times* was that in order to be spectacularly in the right, other people had to be spectacularly in the wrong. If they changed their ground, it undermined their position. Mew would be gratified by evidence of military depravity, disappointed by any sign of reform.

Mew came upon a small flight of broken stone steps leading down to a door of all too human size. A balustrade had, so far, protected the entrance from the worst of the flying snow: even so, a thin coating of white over moss made the steps treacherous. Mew slipped, and fell against the door, which obligingly burst its lock and opened wide. Mew tumbled, as Alice down her well, into a dimly lit corridor. She picked herself up and looked round. She was in a store-place for broken chairs, three-legged tables, torn curtains, unstuffed sofas, butter-spattered tapestries and so forth. Military cadets are famous for their high spirits and jinks, and feel duty bound to live up to their reputation. Things get broken. Joan Lumb would ask the young men, in her introductory lecture to whatever course it was they attended, to do what they could to preserve the dignity and grace of the interior fitments (sic) of the Shrapnel Academy and they would nod and click politely – nothing so polite as a well-educated young gentleman; butter wouldn't melt in his mouth – it was just that when dinner-time came, excitement would surge, drink would be drunk, as often as not from the wrong side of the glass, women being absent private parts would be exposed, and in the general de-bagging, why then butter and potatoes and treacle pudding would fly about the room with the memorial crystal glasses; the tables would be swept clear the better for dancing upon; the sabres on the walls be used for bayoneting sofas – well, in spite, or perhaps because of, everyone's best intentions – the corridor got crowded. And the modern craftsman not being what he was (as the servants were not) and more interested in money than in the exercise of his repairing skills, the corridor seldom got cleared. There was, for the witnessing, a backlog of destruction. Acorn's habit of commandeering household funds for SWORD delayed matters still further. Craftsmen who do not get paid, do not return.

Mew, entering this raggedy, derelict, dimly lit place, was first simply glad to be out of the cold, and then, looking around, aware that this was not the proper entrance for guests. She carried in her pocket, as part of her journalist's equipment, a very small but fool-proof camera, in which she used that kind of film which can pick up images in the almost dark. This she used. Click, click, click again! The camera was no bigger than a key-ring tab.

How Joan Lumb's eyebrows would have raised, had she but known what was happening. What a discourtesy! Photographs ought never to be taken without permission,

especially by the press. But Mew already saw the caption.
'Order on top, chaos below' or some such, and had no
qualms.

Mew opened the door at the end of the corridor, and was
at once in warmth, light and noise. A host of startled eyes
turned towards her. Mew was in the staff dining-room: a
place normally sticky with cooking smells and sweat, noisy
with conversation and the shrieks of playing children. Now
it grew suddenly cold and silent, and the eyes that watched
her were wary. Children scuttled under tables and curled
up and pretended not to exist, as beetles will: old women
melted into the background, as they are so good at doing.
But these ones did it on purpose, and not because they
couldn't help it.

Click, click! It was Mew's instant reaction to untoward
circumstances. Film first, think later.

Neither Acorn nor Inverness were present. Acorn was attending to Murray's glass of tap water and Inverness was
attending to the laying-out of Miriam and her placing in
cold store. When the snow had thawed she would be buried,
with due ceremony, in the staff cemetery at the rear of the
Shrapnel Academy. Others of the senior – that is to say the
English-speaking staff – were for the most part in the kitchens,
busy with the Eve-of-Wellington dinner, and a selected few
upstairs, giving an extra polish to a glass here, straightening
a fork there. Those on the meal shift which Mew now
interrupted were floor scrubbers, groundsmen, porters,
sweepers, those with not sufficient wit to operate domestic
machinery – or assumed not to have it. There was, as
always, soup for dinner: scraps from upstairs bubbled all
day long in ancient stock. The pot never ran dry. The staff
talked, laughed, had good times as well as bad. Everyone
does. Under Acorn's tutelage they were increasingly able to
ignore the religious and dietary differences which so far had
kept them divided. This one Muslim, that one Hindu, that
one Christian, what did it matter? asked Acorn, stirring the

79

pot of their divine discontent to stop it bubbling over when it shouldn't. We have one enemy, only one! Upstairs! No wonder they fell silent, as they now did, at the sight of Mew.

It was left to Raindrop, the houseman, to step forward. He was a small, lean Tamil from Sri Lanka who, alone of his ten-strong family, had escaped death by burning. He had been named Raindrop on a day when Joan Lumb had been feeling on the whole uncreative, but was staring at the rain through an autumnal and melancholy window-pane. He spoke thinly through sensuous lips. He had studied the guest list. This could only be Mew Whittaker.

'Miss Whittaker,' he said, 'I will take you upstairs. They are waiting for you.'

Mew wanted to say, 'But I belong with you. I belong to the poor and oppressed: understand me: let me stay. I am one of the world's victims. I am a woman in a man's world –' but she stayed silent. The stares were too cold, the hostility too evident. She was altogether too white, too well-fed, to make any just claim upon these people. She had the burden of her Imperial past to bear: to be female was not to escape it. She belonged to the world of the mistress, not the maid. She must accept the communal guilt of the lucky. She acquiesced, and followed Raindrop upstairs, not without relief, longing quite badly to be once again where she understood the prevailing rules.

At the top of the stairs, at the green baize door, Raindrop stopped, and passed her over into the care of the waiting Acorn. The gracious rooms, the long corridors, the wide stairways and easy windows of Upstairs were separated from the warren of small rooms and pantries and barred windows of Downstairs by a solid, straight flight of stairs, fourteen treads and fifteen rises high, and a single thick oak door, lined with soft green baize. It could be bolted from either side.

Joan Lumb came forward to greet Mew, strong hand out-stretched. On her forefinger she wore the Shrapnel ring, a fine ruby in a gold setting, which Henry Shrapnel himself had once worn, gift of his monarch, in gratitude for his help in the defence of Gibraltar. Shrapnel's invention, the exploding cannonball, not only put fear into a nation unreasonably claiming the Rock as its own, but was clearly invaluable when a large area had to come under fire from a small. Henry Shrapnel had bequeathed the ring to his grand-daughter; she who had founded the Academy in 1840, to the honour and glory of her grandfather, and the sustenance of the military ethos. Joan Lumb was the tenth Administrator. This was to be the sixtieth Wellington Lecture.

'So you were delayed by the storm, Miss Whittaker?' said Joan Lumb now to Mew. 'Never mind. Just in time! Of course we would have waited dinner! How could we start without *The Times*! You'll want to change. Acorn, take Miss Whittaker to her room on the second floor. Take your time, Miss Whittaker, but not too much. Take your Time! Ha-ha.'
'It's not *The Times* I represent,' said Mew, 'but the *Woman's Times*. It's a new paper, but very good. Feminist, of course.'
'Acorn,' corrected Joan Lumb, 'I meant on the third floor. The Trident Room on the third floor.' She was too well bred to let the expression on her face change. She knew that Acorn would understand. 'Perhaps as you're tired,' she suggested, 'you might prefer to eat in your room tonight?'
'I'm not tired in the least,' said Mew. 'I'll eat with the others.'
What could Joan Lumb do?

Mew followed Acorn upstairs and along long corridors. Marble statues of battling giants, and great vases of dried flowers stood on the first and second landings: even on the third stood naked alabaster ladies, holding lamps. Acorn went ahead.

Acorn wore a black frilled shirt and silk breeches. Over the Wellington Weekend the upstairs staff wore, at Joan Lumb's request, dress which she felt appropriate to the honouring of Henry Shrapnel's life and times.

Acorn, for his part, liked the look of Miss Whittaker. She had, he thought, a good face, albeit white. Mew lived by principle, or tried to, and the very effort carved planes upon her face, as if the granite disc of absolute morality whirred too close for comfort, and shaped her nose straight and firm and her chin strong. She would never be pretty, but she would always be handsome.

'What does she mean "change"?' asked Mew of Acorn when he had opened the door of the small square room which was to be hers, with its single framed photograph of Trident rising from the waves upon the wall, its narrow bed, its white washbasin, table and chair.

'Change for dinner,' explained Acorn, in the gentle, patient tone with which he explained taps, indoor sanitation, knives, forks and shoe laces to those members of the staff who encountered them for the first time. Acorn's capacity for gentleness all but compensated, in the eyes of the staff, for the fits of rage, the all but frothing at the mouth, of which he was also increasingly capable. Joan Lumb, of course, saw only that side of Acorn which he chose to present. 'That means you wash and change and put on fresh clothes before you sit down at the table.'

Mew hopefully searched her rucksack with cracked and grimy hands – she had tried to coax the motorbike into life by fiddling with this and that before realising that its trouble was lack of petrol: and oil, and cold, and the cigarette ash which powdered Edna's car, and dust from the corridor, and the hot greasy atmosphere of the staff kitchen had all left their marks upon her hands and face. She pulled out a crumpled white shirt and said:

'I did bring this. But I'm not one for fancy clothes. I suppose I could iron it. Is there time?'

Acorn said he thought not, and quickly summoned Muffin, who took one look at Mew and all but ran to her own room, El Alamein, and returned with a pink silk blouse, a full red satin skirt, patterned tights and a pair of orange shoes with high heels, and checked that there was soap in Mew's basin.

'I don't mind the skirt,' said Mew. 'Our feeling on the *Woman's Times* is that rather than women aping men and wearing trousers, men should be encouraged to wear skirts. Why should we always give in, and them never? I just love the blouse, so what the hell. But the shoes! To render oneself helpless – madness! Whoever knows what's going to happen next?'

'There isn't time to worry too much,' said Muffin, politely. She felt wonderfully warm and enchantingly sore between her legs: she and Baf's lovemaking had made up for in energy and passion what it lacked in time. 'And look, you have a smear of oil on the side of your face. Don't miss it: I always miss just there by the ear. And do hurry!'

Muffin left. Acorn lingered.

'I won't wear the shoes,' said Mew, stubbornly. 'I'd rather go bare-footed.'

Acorn smiled his slow charming smile and his even white teeth gleamed. Mew could not help but look at his competent hands and imagine them over and in her body, feel his body heavy upon hers – oh, stop it!

'Miss Whittaker,' said Acorn. He took her hand in his and she did nothing to prevent it. She, so easily suspicious of the likes of Baf, was now acquiescent. Perhaps she felt that Acorn, being black, was automatically counted in the number of the oppressed, the good, and so could not be an enemy? Perhaps she had a scale of sexual response, the result of inclination and ideology mixed? It would go like this:

> White women
> Black men
> Black women
> White men

Your author, gentle reader, is not saying good or bad. Your author is just remarking.

'Miss Whittaker,' said Acorn. 'Put on the shoes! Staff come to me in all manner of states. Some will starve rather than eat pork, some will kill rather than not face East at a certain time, some will go mad if they cannot wear a turban, some curl up and die if made to wash in still water. On these trivia, they believe their dignity, their sense of self, their link to past and future depend. They are wrong. Put on the shoes. Join the Family of Nowhere. Bow your head now, the higher to lift it later. Then how great will be your revenge!'

'Tell me more,' said Mew. His hand now held her wrist: he stood close to her: her head came to his chest. The flounces of his black shirt were about her ears.

'Later,' he said, putting her from him as if she were a chocolate and he on a diet. 'Now you must wash and change and put on the shoes, and go down to dinner at once.'

She did so, wondering what he meant by 'later'. She would leave her door unlocked that night; and then observed that anyway there was no lock on the door. In the shadow of the silver Sea-Trident leaping from the water into the cool, clean air, she washed and changed, and within minutes looked truly lovely, being full of vague sexual expectation.

Baf, of course, did not recognise Mew, in her high heels and pink silk, as the girl in the Oxfam scarf by the side of the road, to whom he had so rashly offered a lift. Who could?

18

This was the seating plan for the Eve-of-Waterloo Dinner.

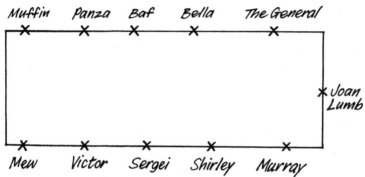

The menu was in honour of Henry Shrapnel, and was based on a dinner served by Mrs Simcoe, wife of the Lieutenant Governor of Upper Canada, in January 1794. (Henry Shrapnel was stationed for a time in Canada.)

Pumpkin Soup

*****

Poached Salmon

*****

Caribou Patties & Cranberry Jelly

*****

Turkey Pie
Sweet Potatoes & Peas

*****

Blueberry Délice

*****

Stilton

The white wine was to be Pouilly Fumé, 1983, and the red a good solid 1976 Margaux. There was to be a ten-year-old Porto Calem with the Stilton. So much one could read on the menu, prettily printed in blue and silver upon white, decorated with a scarlet and gold bow.

The toasts were to be to the Monarch (given by Joan Lumb, responded to by Victor), the Army (given by Murray, responded to by the General), the Shrapnel Academy (given by Victor, responded to by Joan Lumb).

The table staff consisted of Acorn, Rainbow, Yagalone, Horatio, Wendy and Belinda.

There was to be a short programme of music provided by members of the staff, some of whom had come on musical scholarships to this the host country and had then failed to find employment appropriate to their talents; others of whom had enjoyed satisfactory, indeed even splendid musical careers in their native land, but had been obliged to leave for one political or military reason or another.

They were to play, according to the menu, during and after the meal:

Haydn's Quartet in D Major, opus 64, No. 5, The Lark
Three Shanties – Arnold
Quintet in E Minor – Danzi
Mozart's Eine Kleine Nachtmusik K525

The diners were on the whole indifferent to music. Observing this, the musicians played only the Haydn and the Mozart, which they could do, as it were, standing on their heads. Musicians of all races and kinds love to play such little tricks on their audience, when they feel that audience to be uncultured and unresponsive.

Now. People can be known by the way they eat: their characters and their histories; whether they are sensuous or austere, angry or charitable. The child with many siblings

86

guards his food; the oldest eats ravenously; the middle child picks – so busy is he looking from side to side; the youngest eats up, the good little darling! And so forth.

Murray was to toy with his food throughout, leaving most of everything on his plate, although he made some inroads into his salmon.

Bella was to eat ravenously, Murray to watch her, in admiration. So was the General, Baf, Panza, Sergei, and Victor. So was Mew, who was not impervious, as we know, to female charm. Bella was to scrape her plate, mop up her gravy with bread – the cranberry jelly was acceptable though the caribou patty rather tough going, and Bella was hungry, always hungry – and gladly accept more, when Horatio, the one-time harbour pilot from Jakarta, soft-footed and gentle-eyed, appeared at her right elbow with more, the silver dish heavy on a convenient forearm, strong from the guiding of large ships through tricky waters. Bella was, however, to decline the Blueberry Délice and the watching men to decide she did not have a sweet tooth.

Joan Lumb was too busy watching how the food was received to pay much attention to what she ate herself. This is the fate of the hostess. She could only have told you what was in front of her by consulting the menu.

Victor ate happily whatever was on his plate. He and Joan, when children, had been obliged to finish one course before being allowed to go on to the next; not only that – one meal had to be picked clean before the next could begin. Victor had sat, the entire day, on his seventh birthday, before a congealed fried breakfast egg, still not properly set about the yolk, although long since cold and otherwise hard. He knew if he ate the egg he would be sick. At tea-time he did eat it, and was indeed promptly sick. He had a memory of then being required to eat up the sick too, but could not quite believe it. One day he would overcome pain and embarrassment and ask his sister to verify, or otherwise, the memory.

87

But all food nowadays tasted good to Victor, being non-compulsory. He often took second helpings, in order to leave them untouched. Shirley would smile, indulgently.

Shirley was just plain happy to eat a meal she had not prepared herself. She could easily enough have employed a cook, Victor's salary being what it was, but then what sort of wife and mother would she be? How could a family be a family when the food was cooked by an outsider?

Panza ate slowly, chewing every mouthful well, not so much to extract flavour from the food as to do justice by it. He was a short but neatly set man; self-contained: with a straight nose and pretty, almost girlish lips. He was in his late thirties. In his twenties he had been a fencer of Olympic standard: but there the cut and thrust goes to the young and agile: cunning will get you so far, no further. So he had retired from the game, not without bitterness, and lectured instead at the Shrapnel Academy. He understood sport, and endeavour, victory and defeat, as well as the ins and outs of computers. An unusual combination, which made him valuable to the Academy. What is sport, but warfare without blood? What else computers, but thought without guilt?

Sergei ate out of politeness, and the fear of Joan Lumb's vengeance. It was not sensible to offend Joan if there was any way of avoiding it. Little things might happen. He would find his next term's timetable to be full of inconveniences, or the lecture hall allocated to him draughty and with bad acoustics: or the water supply to the summer house dry up, because of the allegedly essential re-laying of water mains in the grounds. These things might only be coincidence: certainly Joan Lumb, if challenged – but who would challenge her? – would deny prejudice let alone malice. Nevertheless Sergei ate and pretended enthusiasm. He would have preferred a quail's egg or two, followed by a strip of veal in Madeira and a green salad, rather than this early Canadian extravaganza of indigestibility. Sergei was a man of taste, discrimination, and judgement. But a patch of alcoholism followed by a bad back and a diet of painkillers led to a brief incarceration in a psychiatric hospital, and after that university and TV work had fallen away; and all there was left was lecturing at Shrapnel and burnt pumpkin soup and Joan Lumb, and whether or not she persecuted him or he merely believed she did, how could he say.

Muffin ate like a well-behaved child.

Mew ate like a bad child: she was sulking: she hated being at the bottom of the table. Conversation was always better at the top.

Baf ate as a young man with a clear conscience eats, ravenously and cheerfully.

The General played with his food. He lifted his soup as if to assist a landing craft, partitioned his patties, piled his potatoes to make an enemy redoubt, sliced slivers off his délice, and ate hardly a thing. His digestion, like Murray's, was not what it had been. Age and anxiety have, in the end, much the same effect as a dose or so of acid.

Sergei smacked his lips over the pumpkin soup.
'Delicious,' said Sergei. 'The real authentic flavour of the redwood bonfire!' He thought he saw Joan Lumb's eyes gleam as if the devil had suddenly peered out from between thunder clouds. Bella lifted her heavy lids and stared at him. He thought her skull was too obvious beneath her skin: the pale eyes looked out from bony sockets. If Joan Lumb was the devil, Bella Morthampton bore a strong resemblance to Death. Sergei looked around the table for some balancing energy, some saving grace, some representation of the Divine, and saw none. The Universe looked black indeed: a kind of Stygian wrinkled cloth, the sort draped over coffins, the weft the grey ordinariness of everyday, the woof malevolence, and not a shiny white thread anywhere, nor any kind of help galloping to the rescue over the celestial horizon to snatch the cloth away. Fortunately the vision

faded before he was half-way through his soup, and he felt better. He was on a course of anti-depressants, and such nightmares were, the doctor told him, not uncommon, though not of an enduring nature. A mere side-effect, in a list which included, in order of frequency reported, nausea, restlessness, lassitude, death.

Throughout the dinner, alliances were formed and enmities established. But today's ally is tomorrow's enemy and vice versa. And the greater enemy, that is to say Downstairs, and the territorial imperative created by the green baize door, had not yet declared itself.

I should perhaps just record here a snatch of conversation between Shirley, Panza and Baf which took place during the soup. Panza wore spectacles with old-fashioned thick glass, and the candlelight kept catching them, so Shirley could hardly see what manner of man he was. His hair was close-cropped.
'I've never seen a man who looked more like a Scorpio!' said Shirley brightly, feeling he needed drawing into the general conversation. 'Do tell me, is your birthday in November?'
'I prefer to keep the date of my birthday to myself,' he said, 'and I am not gullible enough to believe that the stars dictate either my appearance or my nature.'
'Spoken like a Scorpion,' she said. 'I knew it! They'll sting themselves to death rather than admit dependency! You teach computers, I believe? How clever you must be. But then Scorpions are always clever.'
'I do teach the computer sciences,' he said, 'amongst other things.'
'Officers seem to have to know so much,' she said. 'Almost as much as doctors.'
'The professions are not unalike,' he said. 'Both try to prevent death, and both merely hasten it.' Panza's mother had died on the operating table, during an appendectomy. Panza had been five.
'But there's not going to be another war, is there?' she tried

again. 'I mean, there can't be. Mutual deterrence and all that. Isn't that the point?'

'Madam,' he said, 'wars are fought by men, and man does not change. Has there been any discernible difference in the fundamental nature of man over the past five thousand years? No.'

'But surely –' said Shirley.

'That is the one lesson we learn from history,' he said. He did not like questions or interruptions. She was glad not to be one of his students. He turned back to his soup, without enthusiasm.

Shirley turned to Baf. She hoped Piers would grow up to look like this agreeable, cheerful young man. She felt motherly towards him, or thought she did.

'Bet you're a Gemini,' she said. 'May, June?'

'Too right,' he said. 'June 5th. Bang in the middle.'

Baf was in fact born on Christmas Day but knew the value of cheerful lies over the dinner table. Shirley blossomed and preened and he was pleased to see it.

'Now I couldn't possibly have known that, could I?' she said, 'especially as one doesn't usually find Geminis in the army. It's just not an army sign.'

'Actually I'm not in the army,' he said, 'I'm in armaments.'

'Really?' Now she was disconcerted. Nobody liked arms dealers. To make a profit out of death seemed wrong. But here he was at the dinner table just like anyone else. Perhaps she was wrong: perhaps arms dealing was okay?

'Another thing,' said Panza, leaning suddenly towards Shirley, his thin lips ringed with yellow soup. 'Because the nature of man has not changed, neither have his basic objectives when he turns to war: the employment of lethal instruments to force his will upon other men with opposing points of view. War is inevitable.'

He subsided as quickly as he had erupted, and did not speak again for the rest of the meal.

'Wow,' said Baf. 'Quite a speech!' And he smiled at Shirley and Shirley thought, no, I don't feel like his mother, not at all. Why am I dressed like this? In a flowered curtain tied in the middle with a piece of string? Why can't I look like the General's whatever-she-is; why can't I wear a black dress that's so understated it's all statement? She put her spoon down and ate no more soup. Perhaps if she lost weight she would be a different person.

Joan Lumb asked Murray if he was enjoying the music but Murray said he was tone-deaf and lapsed into silence. Baf remarked that being tone-deaf might come in handy in Murray's line of work. There was an interesting new torture being developed in Belfast which involved total sensory deprivation except for three unresolved chords played over and over again.

Joan, who was seldom content with her own seating arrangements, wished she'd seated Baf somewhere altogether further away. He was a pleasant enough young man; but like all the young of today, had no sense of what was in bad taste and what was not. But Murray seemed not to have heard what Baf said, or at any rate did not reply, and fortunately the General seemed interested, if sceptical, rather than offended. He and Baf liked one another.

'But does it work?' asked the General, 'or is it like so many of these new ideas? Fine in theory but hopeless in the field?' And he told the story of the USS *Princeton*, the first screw-propelled warship in the world. A certain Robert F. Stockton, a US navy captain, devised a new 12-inch gun for the *Princeton*, named it 'The Peacemaker'; fitted it, and steamed down the Potomac to try it out. The gun looked just fine on paper. But when it was fired it blew up, killing the Secretary of State, the Secretary of the Navy, and several Congressmen besides, all of whom had turned out to see the fun. Oh, the fun of it, 'til it stopped. What a bang! Whose bits went into which coffin was anyone's guess.

'Fine in theory but not in practice,' concluded the General. Baf said the Belfast trials hadn't been concluded yet: time would tell. Shirley asked if it wasn't odd to call a gun

'Peacemaker', but Joan Lumb said briskly that it was not odd at all: war existed to preserve peace. She signalled to Acorn, who gestured to his staff, who removed the empty soup plates. That is to say, some were empty, some merely finished with. Pumpkin soup can be a little sickly sweet for some tastes, and it had, in the making, gone through some vicissitude.

My own opinion where pumpkins are concerned is that the only way to eat the stuff is very fresh, cut up small, and served as a vegetable. Forget pumpkin pie, forget pumpkin soup. Toss pieces of pumpkin in melted butter in a hot pan, salt, cover with boiling water, simmer briefly, drain well, and serve with more butter and ground pepper. Then it's just fine – a cross between old courgette and new potato. Leave out the butter if you worry about the cholesterol, the salt if your blood pressure's high, the pepper if you worry about carcinogens. (It's not, these days, so much that we fiddle while Rome burns, as we chatter away, exchanging recipes and tips on healthy living.)

After the soup, two whole poached salmons were presented to the guests, each on its own silver plate, one at each end of the table. They were noble fish, albeit dead. Acorn presented one at Joan Lumb's end of the table: Raindrop the other, at Mew and Muffin's end. This latter fish, Sergei observed, was on the whole inferior in colour and texture, being the product of a fish farm and not of a Canadian mountain stream. The fish were then whisked away to be not so much carved as partitioned – for who can carve a really fresh salmon? The flesh is too tender; it disintegrates beneath the knife. A delicate cucumber salad was served with the fish. This had been properly made: the cucumber peeled and salted, blanched with boiling water, crisped immediately with iced water, well drained, and the now limp yet lively slices tossed in a delicate vinaigrette. The bread rolls that went with the fish and salad were home-made, soft, puffy and warm.

Joan Lumb was pleased to see, after the all-but failure of the soup, that the fish was well received. She blamed Mrs Simcoe in her heart, not only for putting up with such a terrible soup, but actually recording the recipe. Mrs Simcoe, of course, had had trouble with the servants: Upper Canada was one of the worst places for servants in the world, she wrote home at the time. 'We cannot get a woman who can cook a Joint of Meat unless I am at her heels . . . I have a Scotch girl from the Highlands, Nasty, Ill-tempered Creature.' Joan Lumb felt sorry for Mrs Simcoe, as must any woman for another who has servant trouble, however far in the past that trouble might be, but by now mistrusted her judgement, and fear as to how the caribou patties would turn out quite spoiled her pleasure in the success of the fish.

It was over the fish that Mew engaged Victor in a discussion about abortion, and incurred his dislike.
'What do you think of the new abortion law?' Mew asked him. There are always new abortion laws, as societies struggle over the meaning of life and death.
'I don't think,' said Victor, 'it's a subject I want to talk about over dinner.'
Mew looked puzzled.
'Then when would you want to talk about it?'
'Actually,' he said, 'not at all. Any more than I want to talk about murder.'
'I suppose you think murder and abortion are the same thing!' said Mew.
'My dear young lady,' said Victor. 'I have no doubt that you are all for abortion and the strangling of defective babies at birth and so on and so forth, but please, not over the fish!'
'Over the caribou patty, then,' said Mew. 'And anyway I'm not sure about strangling; I imagined smothering is preferable. Less violent.'
At this point Victor turned away rather pointedly to talk to Sergei, on his right. What could possibly have induced his sister to ask this disagreeable young woman to dinner?

94

'Don't you think it odd,' said Mew to Muffin, loudly, 'that people who view the destruction of fully grown millions with equanimity should get so concerned about the fate of a wretched foetus or so?'

But Muffin, wisely, refused to be drawn into the conversation; she smiled and nodded agreeably and Mew sighed and went back to her fish, and planned questions in her mind for her interview with the General. She was surprised that he seemed so personable and equable: she had expected a twitchier and more wizened person by far. It occurred to her that the fork in her hand was both pleasant to the touch and nicely balanced and she concluded that it was made of pure silver.

'Where does the Shrapnel Academy get its funding?' she asked Muffin.

'What do you mean?'

'How do you pay everyone's wages?'

'Out of the bank, of course,' said Muffin.

'How does it get into the bank?' asked Mew.

'You'd have to ask Joan Lumb that,' said Muffin, primly.

'I will,' said Mew. Muffin was sorry she had lent Mew her clothes and decided she did not like her one bit.

Victor asked Sergei, courteously, what his function at the Academy was. Sergei replied that he taught Liberal Studies to the cadets. The army liked its officers to have a broad cultural base. The Ancient World could teach the modern a great deal about the government of the apparently ungovernable, the handling of subject tribes, the suppression of subversion, and so forth. The modern soldier must be able to do more than merely defend his shores.

'After all,' said Sergei, 'in any future conflict it's likely that the central civilian power will collapse almost at once. Its representatives are elected, not promoted, and for all the wrong reasons. It would be left to the army to take over the chain of command: soldiers must know how to govern.'

95

Victor said that surely business executives would have the requisite training to take over a panicked and indecisive government in time of nuclear crisis, and there was more than enough of them about to do so.

'Business executives are trained to compete,' said Sergei, flatly, 'not to co-operate. They would not be suitable.'

And he engaged Victor's reluctant attention on a matter dear to him, on certain rumours circulating in the classicist community, relating to the burning down of the library at Alexandria in the year AD 304.

Victor looked over at Bella, and speculated as to whether she closed her eyes or kept them open while she made love. Shirley kept hers closed, except when (or so Victor supposed) she remembered a passage in *The Art of Loving* and kept them open by an effort of will.

Shirley, even as he wondered, leant over to him and said, 'Do you think the children are all right?'

'Why don't you go and see?' said Victor. So Shirley did. She slipped away between the fish and the caribou patty.

Sergei went on talking to Victor about the library at Alexandria. It was, he said, the greatest library the world had ever known; its burning down was rated by the knowledgeable people as one of the Great World Disasters. Some contemporary historians, however, now maintained that the library had not in fact burned down at all. What happened was that the rich citizens of Alexandria, being under siege, had burned whole sections of manuscript in order to keep their central heating working. This was the reason that most of all known classical writers have their names at the beginning of the alphabet or the end. Aristotle, Aeschylus, Sophocles, Socrates – those in the middle are missing, burned. What did Victor think?

Victor said politely that it sounded to him like a plot by a Marxist historian to discredit people with central heating. Art, as everyone knew, was preserved by the rich, not the poor. This had the ring of a typical atrocity story: something hard to disprove, founded on a grain of truth, and dear to the heart of the listener. Sergei shouldn't let it worry him. Victor thought that Sergei was probably quite mad. If Sergei sat before him at an appointments board he would not employ him. You could tell from the soft slack mouth that he was an idealist, a man of indecision and impractical ideas. Victor wondered what could possibly have induced Joan to have him on the staff.

19

Shirley went up to Genghis Khan and found Hilda still
Sitting dutifully on a hard chair by Piers' bed. The three
children slept soundly, their curly heads damp, bedclothes
up to their ears. Hilda's pretty brown hands, with their
elegant almond nails, were composed in her lap. It always
annoyed Shirley that the help's hands were so often more
acceptable than her own large floppy ones, which, however
conscientiously she gloved and creamed, remained red and
chapped.

'Can't you see they're too hot,' she said crossly, busily
removing blankets.

'It is so cold outside!' said Hilda, and indeed the blizzard
now howled outside the window, as if some furious com-
plaining giant prowled without, clamouring to get in. The
windows of Genghis Khan, alone of all on the first floor,
were not double-glazed. The outside world was only a thin
pane of glass away.

'That doesn't make it cold in here, does it!' remarked
Shirley, and even as she spoke was ashamed of the sneering
tone she heard coming from her own lips. But it was always
the same: in defence of her own interests she was too soft
and mild, in defence of the children too hard and sharp.

'Perhaps now they are asleep I should go downstairs?' asked
Hilda.

'They might wake and be frightened,' said Shirley. 'I'd
rather you stayed.' That, after all, said the tone of her voice,
is what you are paid for.

And Shirley went downstairs without further comment from
Hilda, and rejoined the dinner party.

'Just as well I went,' she said to Victor. 'They were much
too hot. What an idiot the girl is! Joan is mad to trust

non-Europeans. What can they possibly know about child care?' It was a rhetorical question. Victor didn't reply. He wasn't concentrating. He didn't suppose that Bella had ever had children, or would even want to.

Now, reader, while we are on the subject of the neglected and ignored, that is to say both Shirley and Hilda in their own way, for these things are handed on down the scale of emotional underprivilege, which in my mind at least goes –

White men
Black men
White women
Black women
Animals

– you may be wondering about the dog, Harry. We last saw him at the opening of the novel, staring out at the snow-flakes melting against the heated rear window of the Blades' Volvo. Joan Lumb had the animal taken down to the servants' quarters the minute he arrived. Neither Shirley nor Victor had protested much at being separated from their dog – he was the organic division of Security's otherwise inorganic and electronic plan for the safety of the Blade family, rather than a pet. With Harry in the back of the car, their reasoning was, kidnap attempts on the children were not so likely. At the first sign of trouble, a button on the steering wheel would lower the dog mesh, and Harry would be in there, attacking the attackers, and one hoped not the children! Shirley and Victor very much admired the animal's style and looks, and felt a responsibility for him, but it was difficult to feel fond of him. Shirley was better at it than Victor, and was often heard to say, 'Good dog, Harry! What a beautiful animal you are! How nice it is for the children to have a pet!' and so forth.

When Shirley returned from seeing the children, and had recovered a little from Victor's apparent non-interest in their welfare, she pulled herself together and joined in the general conversation. A dog, at the very least, is always a talking point.

'So much is a matter of terminology,' the General was saying. 'I used to work for the Ministry of War. Now it's the Ministry of Defence. Same place, same people, different name.'

'For peace read war,' said Baf. 'When I hear the word peace I reach for my gun. I know I'm going to have to defend myself.'

The General and Baf laughed uproariously. They were getting on like a house on fire, like a house exploding, like a nuclear blast. Talking of which, when the physicists from Los Alamos let off the first atomic bomb in New Mexico, in 1945, nobody really knew what would happen. Some of them thought the blast might set off a chain reaction which would destroy all matter, that is to say the world. Some of them thought the reaction would stop after a time and destroy only the state of Nevada. Those ones left in a hurry. The more optimistic just stood off five miles, crossed their fingers, pressed the button, and hoped. There was first a cloud of dust, then a swirling inferno, then an enormous, wonderful bang, a glorious mushroom cloud, and a two-mile crater. They'd got it right! Well, roughly. And they weren't down-wind, so they didn't get the fall-out. They didn't know about fall-out, until the cattle and sheep and people down-wind lay down and died, but it made the new weapon even more interesting and likely to win the war, so they dropped one first on Hiroshima and then on Nagasaki, both cities having been kept un-bombed all through the war so as to provide a clean testing ground, and then sent in teams of scientists after it. These latter were really nice men, good guys, and met no opposition, no hostility. They remarked upon that and could make no sense of it. In order to be good guys you have to meet up with bad guys. Anyway, enough of all this. More plaintive civilian whines! They were great exciting days at Los Alamos and the frontiers of knowledge were pushed well and truly back by Oppenheimer, the future's equivalent to Henry Shrapnel, inventor of the exploding cannonball.

'Well,' said Shirley, 'if you can call a gun Peacemaker, I'm going to call Harry the dog peacebarker!'

And everyone laughed some more, and Victor felt quite proud of his wife, and even Joan Lumb seemed to approve.

'Harry's a walking defensive weapon,' said Victor.

'If he bit you you'd describe him as offensive,' said Panza, who found life down the end of the table boring and kept craning his powerful neck to join in.

'Well, anyway,' said Shirley, 'all I hope is he's all right down there with the servants. You know what these people are. Some of them actually eat dog!'

Now dogs are indeed eaten in many parts of the world, but in the same civilised and ritual manner that lambs and cows are eaten in our own. Shirley did not know this. How could she? She had a vague feeling that the living animal would be seized up, wrenched apart, and the warm flesh devoured uncooked without benefit of knife and fork, and the tender raw bones chewed upon, and that would be the end of Harry.

It was unfortunate that just as she expressed her fear that Peacebarker would be eaten, Acorn was bending over her right shoulder serving the cranberry jelly which went with the caribou patty (and how rubily red and rich it looked, rather like congealed blood) and the method of his revenge was made clear to him. He would hesitate no longer. Oppression, poverty, hardship, even the violation of human rights can be put up with, in the search for at best a quiet life, at the least survival. It is the wilful stupidity of the master races which in the end cannot be borne. It is their unreasonable assumption of moral superiority which proves intolerable. Miriam had died that day. Her death was at the diners' hands. Downstairs was restive. Inverness might yet prove a real danger. The scales must be righted. A gesture must be made.

Acorn finished serving up the jelly, went downstairs (leaving Rainbow in charge) and summoned Inverness.

'Kill the dog. Stew it.'

Inverness's eyes gleamed from behind his thick glasses. So Zia, one evening in 1975, had spoken of Bhutto.

'Is this wise?' he asked.

'A life for a life,' said Acorn. 'They hold their pets dearer than they do their servants.'

Miriam lay wrapped in silver foil upon a shelf in the cold store. When the snow cleared she would be buried in the old pets' cemetery which had existed for hundreds of years in a clearing of the Shrapnel woods. Here some twelve of the staff lay: long human bones, sturdy human skulls, in amongst tiny cat jaws, little lap-dog thighs, delicate monkey fingers.

'But where will it end?' pleaded Inverness. 'One atrocity begets another.'

'Let us not think of endings,' said Acorn, grandly, to considerable applause from those who had gathered to listen, 'when we haven't even begun.'

It is doubtful whether at this point Acorn really wanted all-out war. Few war historians are ever certain of this point. Does this nation or that really want war? Does this husband, this wife, *really* want divorce? It's just the way one thing leads to another, in marriage as in war. This unfortunate remark – calculated or even casual, as Shirley's was – leading to that act of revenge: this saving of face leading to that punitive action – and before you know where you are the children are homeless, crying in the streets, either in their hearts or in real life, and everything's banging and popping all around. Why I make a distinction between 'the heart' and 'real life' I can't imagine. The heart *is* real life.

And of course, as Inverness so boringly pointed out, Acorn's act of retaliation, the first definite act of war, was not altogether a wise one. It is better to start a war with a deed which can easily be attributed to the enemy. Your side then has the moral ascendancy throughout the conflict: that is to say 'we didn't start this, you did, yah, yah, yah –' and fights the better for it. Or, as Napoleon said more loftily, 'the moral is to the physical as three is to one'. But sometimes indignation overwhelms prudence. Acorn had not been formally trained in military matters – apart from one summer holiday spent learning the practical arts of guerilla warfare for SWORD – but in law; and in life, in the school of general hardship and upset. But that does not help. Those who sit on soft cushions and live politely and eat well and play war games, have the advantage in energy and cunning over those who starve and suffer and are bitter. Everything's so much easier when it's fun! Everything goes better if you don't take it seriously. On the other hand, Downstairs has a vast superiority in numbers over Upstairs and the advantage of surprise and an inbuilt system of informers – well, we will see.

Upstairs, the caribou patties were, to be frank, a little stringy. The meat had been flown over from Canada, marinated, as caribou should be, in a mixture of claret, brandy and the animal's own blood (vacuum packed for the journey in a tough plastic sachet), then simmered in the marinade with a bouquet garni in a very low oven indeed. The flesh should then all but have tenderly disintegrated. Unfortunately this particular animal had led a wilder and randier life than most, and was unusually tough. Raindrop had to almost pulverise the meat to get it to a consistency which mixed well with the egg yolk and spices Mrs Simcoe's recipe required, and the result was both stringy to the teeth and floury to the tongue, though no flour was of course used in the making. (No good cook ever thickens with flour; he reduces, or uses a little tomato puree.) The flavour was excellent, but the texture failed. Joan Lumb wondered if she should fire Raindrop, and thought perhaps she would. It kept the staff on their toes, to dismiss one or two from time to time, when things went wrong.

Muffin picked at her patty and wondered why she had lost her appetite and decided it was because Baf was talking animatedly, and making people laugh, and she thought he was doing it for Bella's benefit.

'Do you know the General's secretary?' Muffin asked of Mew.

'No,' said Mew. 'Thank God. I don't move in army circles.'

Muffin rubbed an itchy place on her chin and realised she was growing a pimple. Bella Morthampton might (and might well, from the look of her) die of consumption but would never be afflicted by anything as absurd as a spot. Bella wore a plain black dress. Muffin was wearing rather a lot of pink flounces. She hated herself.

'Of course she isn't his secretary, at all,' said Muffin to Mew, rashly. 'Everyone knows she's his mistress. Bella Morthampton's famous. She started off in the Ministry of Defence canteen, and has gone up and up, that is to say older and older, ever since.'

'Really!' said Mew, and took something small and black from inside the elasticated cuff of the sleeve of her blouse (not hers at all, of course, but Muffin's) and pointed it down the table. Click! Click! 'Army Sex Scandal! General's Sexual Toy!'

But that's a camera, Muffin thought. She's taking photographs.

'You can't do that!' said Muffin.

'Why not?'

'It isn't done.'

'Surely no one here has anything to be ashamed of?'

'But you're a *guest*. This is *dinner*!'

'Of course, if it upsets you –'

Mew put the camera away, having done with it all that she needed to. Click! Click! 'Low wages lead to life of degradation! Sexual exploitation of canteen workers!'

'Thanks,' said Muffin, feeling a little sheepish at having made a fuss. But since her mother and father had died, Joan Lumb and the Academy had taken their place, and she felt she had to be loyal. She wished she could explain this to Mew, but how could she begin?

The caribou patty finished, turkey pie was served. The General would have preferred plain roast turkey, which was his favourite, but this would do. The young man on his right, whom he so liked, now seemed to be trying to sell him something. What was he saying? A flame thrower you could hold in the palm of your hand? Life moved ahead so quickly these days, it was hard to keep up.

For life, as it were, read death.

For peace, as Baf keeps saying, read war.

20

Now. Let us go back a little in time. When Harry arrived
at the Shrapnel Academy he was taken downstairs and shut
in a disused laundry room, together with a bowl of water.
He went amiably enough. He recognised, when he saw it,
a definite chain of command – and this one went from Victor
to Shirley to Joan Lumb to Blackthorne – into whose care
Joan Lumb had placed him, with the obvious consent of
Victor, who stood placidly by while he, Harry, was led
away. Each transaction the dog noted, and accepted. All
these people he could now include in the list of non-enemies
(Harry did not aspire to actual *friends*) and the more non-
enemies he had the better. If anyone attacked one of his
non-enemies, they would then become enemies and fair
play for what he most loved doing – growling, crouching,
bristling, leaping, biting, tearing, rending, throwing living
flesh in all directions, and all in legitimate defence of the
non-enemy. Keeping the peace! Oh, terrific!

Harry settled down to sleep on the blanket provided – if a
dog has nothing else to do it sleeps, and the laundry room
was swept, scoured and empty and devoid of interest – when
presently the door opened and a certain young woman,
Agnes, was pushed inside. Agnes was a used and abused
ex-child-prostitute from Korea. When Agnes wept, groaned
or showed her private parts too often and too much it was
the staff's custom to shut her away for a time until she
regained her composure. And no doubt this community care
was a better alternative for Agnes than any offered in the
world outside: that is to say, if not deported, then drugged
and locked up in some secure hospital for lunatics. Which
Agnes plainly was: it could not be denied that she had
finally, while in the Shrapnel Academy, lost her wits.

Joan Lumb had taken Agnes on in her better, more lucid days, to be the girl who cleaned out the upstairs lavatories. It had soon become clear that Agnes was not fit for upstairs work. She upset the young gentlemen by popping her stolid head round corners and smiling and beckoning, when they had other things on their mind, and even if they hadn't, certainly wouldn't wish to make do with the likes of Agnes. Now, if it had been Muffin, or Hilda, smiling and beckoning that would have been another story. As it was, complaints were blushingly made.

So Agnes lost her job; that is to say, Joan Lumb fired her, and assumed her to have packed her bags and gone. Of course she merely did without her wages and joined the other illegal occupants living in the servants' quarters of the Shrapnel Academy off the scraps of the upstairs' table. Where else was she to go?

Agnes, disturbed by the changing atmosphere of the staff quarters, by the increasing mutterings for revenge and justice, had done what she always did when upset – that is to say, taken off all her clothes and smiled. She was pushed unceremoniously into the laundry room, to stay there until she felt better. Hastings, from the Philippines, an electrician by trade but now a gardener, did the pushing, unaware that Harry, or Peacebarker, was already occupying the room. He pushed Agnes into the dark and switched on the light only as he closed the door behind her. If she was left in the dark she would sometimes start screaming.

Harry opened his eyes and stared at Agnes. Agnes sat down in her normal crouching position and stared back. Harry was tired and he had been fed. He shuffled and snuffled, decided Agnes was a non-enemy and went back to sleep. His body seemed warm, soft and indifferent, so Agnes moved over and lay against him and went to sleep too. The room was not particularly warm: the central heating system at the Academy (oil-fired) did magnificently for the upper floors, but here down below was only just adequate. But

107

then, why should it not be so? Servants cannot expect to live so well as masters.

Presently the door opened and Yew entered. Yew came from the Bombay Police Force, from which he had been dismissed for putting out the eyes of suspects with bicycle spokes. In one hand Yew carried an open can of dog food: in the other he carried a long, curving, sharp dagger.

I don't know why it seems worse to put out eyes with bicycle spokes than by any other means, but it does. Which is why, of course, that kind of thing's done. Terror is an excellent means of crowd control, as the Assyrians discovered long ago. Of course civilisation has come a long way since then. It is greatly to the credit of the Indian authorities that Yew was dismissed from his post (the Assyrians would merely have promoted him), and less, how shall we put it, *vivid* ways of crime prevention re-introduced. His ways, of course, were more effective. They do, incidentally, say that after ten years of chopping off the hands of Iranian thieves, it is now possible for a vendor of gold bracelets in that country to set them out on the ground in a crowded market, go away, and find them all there, untouched, when he returns hours later. I offer this to you only as a piece of interesting information: I don't expect you to come to any conclusions. I suspect there are none to come to. None at least satisfactory to the humane spirit.

Well, Harry, Agnes and Yew. This is how the scene goes. Harry opens his eyes. Harry is no fool. He knows a defensive weapon when he sees one. He'll have to beware. It practically has 'Peace' written all over it. That is to say, Harry's eternal peace. Harry stands, throwing off Agnes, effortlessly. He's a really big, sinewy dog, who grew from a puppy into, with a little help on the way, a war machine. Harry snarls, growls. Yew wishes he had something longer than the dagger, such as a bicycle spoke. But bicycle spokes are too flexible: good for eyes; not right for piercing hair and skin. Harry takes no notice at all of the dog food. Yew tosses the can away and stands crouching, wary, arms akimbo, the dagger poised, waiting for Harry to spring. Harry doesn't: Harry circles.

Agnes slips out of the door. Yew, distracted, looks after her briefly: Harry chooses the moment to spring from the back; Yew has grossly underestimated his victim. Harry, unlike the citizens of Bombay, is simply not scared of Yew. It is easier to frighten a human being than a dog. A healthy-minded dog attacks to preserve his master, or his territory. That his master may be Hitler makes no difference to him: that the territory is disputed, how can he know? (Up go the bristles, off goes the dog, and there's the postman refusing to deliver the letters, the milkman to leave the milk!) But a human being is all doubts as to the rights and wrongs of anything and everything: guilt paralyses him. The inquisitor advances; he scarcely needs the thumb-screws: the soul shrinks, resolve weakens. But Harry, being a dog and guilt-less, and what's more the kind of dog who reckons he's man's equal, sprang at Yew's shoulders without hesitation, bore him to the ground and, had not Yew instantly crouched in that position children are taught to assume under desks in case of nuclear or terrorist attack, would have had his throat torn out. As it is, from this position, while Harry noses and nuzzles towards available flesh, Yew manages to manoeuvre his dagger so that the dog's soft and almost hairless belly is first lightly pierced: then, as the animal twists to see what the matter is, Yew turns on his side, gets his elbow free, jabs harder and rips. The dog's entrails fall out: it is all perfectly disgusting. Yew is on his back now, and the dog is moaning and groaning and falling all over him, but hasn't quite forgotten about enemies and so forth, because he dies self-righteously growling his antagonism, not moaning his own pain, his fate. When it is over Yew is in a very nasty, bloody state indeed and goes to have a shower, and to calm his mind by meditating for five minutes before Kali's shrine (set up in one of the pantries) before returning to skin the dog, which he does with the ease born of practice. He carves the carcass into pieces, and places the haunches here, rump there, in mimicry of the living animal, in a long wicker basket which he brings in for the purpose. The poor dull-eyed handsome head he places at one end. He carves out the tongue: this is a delicacy he will reserve for Acorn. He carries the basket, and its still warm contents, into the kitchen and sends for Matilda the Mexican girl to wash out the laundry room. Matilda is used to death, and does what Yew says. Most people do.

Barnyard the Chinese chef prepares a simple *bouillon* in which the chunks of dog are immersed and simmered. There is no time to waste if the meat is to be properly tenderised and reduced to pâté in time for the late-night sandwiches. These are to be served with cocoa at around midnight. The meat ought of course to be properly marinated before being cooked. Hilda, who has briefly left her post at the bedsides of Serena, Piers and Nell to have a whiff of marijuana – the smell would be noticeable and unnatural upstairs, though ordinary enough down here – and look at poor Miriam's new baby, which is being suckled by Olive, whose own baby is nine months old and ready for weaning, protests at this lack of decorum. What way of cooking meat is this? It is an insult to the animal concerned, and the palate of those who eat it. A marinade of soya sauce, chilli and fresh ginger would sanctify the death. Why can't the guests have the pâté tomorrow, served on toast, if necessary, for breakfast? Why does it have to be in the sandwiches served with the late-night cocoa? Why, in other words, is Acorn in such a hurry? What are his plans?

No one knows. They will simply do as Acorn says. The dog is dead, the deed is done: too late now not to go on. Harry simmers.

Hilda weeps a little; big tears welling slowly in her lovely eyes. She fears that Acorn's project is ill-omened. No plan can go properly if started in such an improper way. But what can she do? The blizzard now howls round the Shrapnel Academy as if there were not just one but a hundred demons outside clamouring to get in. She's frightened. She throws a handful of cumin and some fresh ginger into the pot and says a brief prayer over it and goes back upstairs, into enemy territory, to sit by the sleeping white children. She walks slowly and calmly, into terror, not away from it. She is accustomed to hardship: it is more natural to her to endure, than to be comfortable.

21

Over the turkey pie Baf gave the General a brief rundown
on the contents of his Victorian knife box, and the General
said he'd like to have a look at it, later, but Baf should be
aware that purchasing decisions were in much loftier hands
than his.

'But you can recommend,' said Baf.

'Oh, I can recommend,' said the General. 'But who takes
note of old soldiers these days? It's politicians who rule the
roost, not to mention accountants. No one's in charge any
more who's actually seen battle.'

Well, it's a common enough complaint, these days. The
money men run everything, and they know nothing about
the world, only about money.

Baf made the General the little speech he made to generals
and War Departments everywhere, but preferably where
English was either a first or second language. It tended to
lose in the translation: or else it was that the non-English
speaking nations were less interested in theory than in
eliminating their enemies – or obliging them to talk. As well
as his range of miniaturised weapons, Baf had a second line
of torture instruments. He hadn't told Muffin this: he felt
vaguely ashamed of being in the business, although ration-
ally there was nothing against it. If men chose to be enemies
of the state, the state had a right to protect itself. Anyone,
anywhere, who wanted a quiet life only had to choose it,
by keeping their noses out of trouble and refraining from
comment. And the export of these instruments made quite
a useful bump in the national balance of payments. All the
same Baf thought that Muffin, who, if out of doors, would
stop in mid-lovemaking to rescue a woodlice which got in

the way, would not be in sympathy with his new range of sensory deprivation hoods, electric vagina probes, and so on. Yet there was nothing brutal or brutish about them, Baf felt. The days of the rack and bottle dungeons were over: a good contemporary inquisitor leaves no mark on the body for soft-hearted and impractical liberals to complain about. And this was, after all, the age of information. Information, as people kept saying, was money, power. Those who chose to keep it inside their heads in defiance of the national interest had to expect to have it wrested from them, by hood, or probe, or whatever, as quickly and efficiently as possible. Baf's speech went, in essence, like this:

'Well now, General, look at it like this. New weapons get invented, leaving armies out of step and battles bloody and unfair. It happened when gunpowder came on the scene – one army had it, another didn't – the same with the rifled musket, then with automatic weapons, high explosives and nuclear weapons – and presently there will be chemical weapons and coming up fast on the outside, miniaturised weapons. Those who get these latter first will have the advantage. The great thing about them is that they're *individual*. Now the individual soldier has become increasingly independent in combat, he already has to be a technician: sheer muscle power, brawn, courage are no longer needed. A good modern soldier runs away when danger faces – he knows he's too expensive to lose! Now since time began – or armies began, much the same thing, ha-ha! – there have always been new weapons just on the horizon, and a lot of money spent by the forward-looking on R and D – it's been getting them accepted – the doctrinal assimilation of new weapons into tactical systems – has been the trouble. By the time any new weapon – whether a cannonball or a nuclear blast – gets assimilated, word's got round and the enemy have learned how to disperse, run for cover, burrow underground. So the impact of that weapon, its destructive power, is lessened. In other words, General, move fast! Or you'll miss out.

113

'Now fortunately, the pace of military invention more or less keeps pace with what's being developed in the outside world; though that's certainly been hotting up lately. Look at those Russian probes burrowing into Venus in a temperature of 700°F! And the gap between invention and adoption of a new weapon gets shorter all the time.'

'Wait a moment,' said the General, who was no fool, though only listening with half an ear. With the other half he was listening to Shirley; he liked her voice. She was, he thought, rather pretty and gentle. There was something so sacred and unsmiling about Bella, so profane about his sexual relations with her, that the General felt quite restive and longed for something just somehow more ordinary and domestic. Fortunately he could keep his mind on two things at once. It's a capacity generals have. They share it with mothers. 'New weapons don't normally appear in operations until twenty years or so after a major war,' said the General to Baf. 'It's inevitable because of budgetary and stockpile considerations. The old ones have to be utilised, if only for face-saving reasons. Also because men like me, who made their name in a big war, see nothing wrong with simply going on using the old weapons, since they did them well enough in the past. You have to wait for me to grow old and the bright young men to come along. Try one of them. Leave me to eat my dinner in peace.'

'Sir,' said Baf, 'if we take the criteria of judging a new weapon to be its consistently effective, flexible use in defensive warfare, permitting full exploitation of the advantages of superior leadership; if a decline in casualties for those who use it, combined with a capacity for inflicting disproportionately heavy losses on the enemy is what you're after, then this new range of miniaturised weapons splendidly fits the bill! All that is lacking, until now, is the imaginative component, knowledgeable leadership, that you, sir, will provide, to your country's eternal gratitude!'

'Humph!' said the General. 'What's missing, if you ask me, is any opportunity for evaluation and analysis on the battleground.'

'If you don't try it,' said Baf, 'you'll never know.'
'Young man,' said the General, 'there's a time and place for this kind of thing, and it isn't the dinner table.'
'Don't tell Joan Lumb,' said Baf disarmingly, 'that I've been pestering you, or she'll never ask me here again. And I have to come here, to see Muffin.'

He smiled at the General, his soft brown eyes crinkling, and the General smiled back.
'Is Muffin the one with the legs and the hair?' he asked.
'That's her, sir.'
'Wouldn't want to stand between a man and his muffin,' said the General. 'Mum's the word. We'll talk after breakfast tomorrow. I'll give you a name or two at the War Office which should help. You may be on to something here.'

Most deals are done at dinner. Would you oblige me by trying to envisage the Délice? It was in the form of a cannon. The muzzle was made of ice-cream wound round a chocolate stick and frozen hard. The hump of the Délice itself was made of whipped cream, blueberry purée and gelatine frozen hard. The words, THE SHRAPNEL ACADEMY, were written around its girth in icing sugar. It wasn't very nice. Rosencrantz the pastry chef, a Mexican Indian, had added rather too much gelatine, in his fear of not sustaining the cannon's shape and the result was, though spectacular to the eye, rubbery to the taste. Joan Lumb, actually, had very little palate, or she would never have devised anything so absurd as a Délice shaped like a cannon. It was impossible to serve fairly, and collapsed at the first spooned inroad. The plain fact of the matter is that army people are not really connoisseurs of life's pleasures. Put them in an insti-tution and the fault intensifies. Put them in an educational establishment and things are even worse. Wake me up in front of a plate, rather too small for its contents, on which are a dried-out baked chicken leg, a pool of grey gravy, an ice-cream scoop of mashed potato barely holding its shape, and a tumble of frozen peas and carrots mixed without favour of butter or seasoning, and I can tell at once I am in an educational institution and what is worse they are doing their very best and what is worst, is that this for them is a treat. A treat. This lack of reverence for the pleasures of the palate, this inability to discriminate between good and bad, helps no one, not the starving millions either, for the food is simply spoiled, not passed on to those who could use it for nourishment rather than ceremony – and is symptomatic, I suspect, of those who care little for life, their own or anyone else's. This is why I go on about it, in what to you may seem a rather vulgar way. In my grandmother's day, I know, it was bad form to talk about, discuss or mention food – the food was appalling, and the poor stumbled shoeless and starving in the gutters outside and nobody cared. I am just making a connection. If you wish to conclude anything, feel free.

With the coffee came the toast. Glasses were refilled. Joan Lumb responded to the toast 'The Shrapnel Academy'. She said she was moved and inspired by the occasion. That she was honoured and gratified by the presence here that night of General Leo Makeshift. That from what he had been saying to her it was clear his annual lecture was going to be historic. All 200 of tomorrow's tickets had been sold: there was a growing interest in the military ethos amongst young and old. The civil government was in disarray: strife and subversion were rampant in the world today: the traditions of the past were enshrined here in the Shrapnel Academy. Mew yawned. Joan Lumb noticed.

Joan Lumb said she wanted to take this opportunity to clear up a misconception. It was unfortunate that over the years all shell-fragment wounds had come to be called 'shrapnel wounds'. This was in fact incorrect terminology. She explained. In the late eighteenth and early nineteenth century grapeshot was the principal anti-personnel ammunition. Grapeshot consisted of a packet of small iron balls held together by cloth, or netting, placed in a wooden case. This would then be fired from a cannon. But it had shortcomings – as all weapons do: hence the eternal search for improvement – it had a very short range and the advancing enemy could take advantage of undulating territory and take cover. It was Shrapnel's stroke of genius to make the balls smaller than was usual for grapeshot, to make them of lead, not iron, and encase them in a long-fused cannonball shell. This completely overcame the disadvantages of grapeshot. It could be fired over a considerable distance, would explode in the air, and troops could not hide from pellets raining from the sky.

Still there were difficulties. A new set of problems had to be overcome. It required a highly trained gunner to combine range, direction and height of burst over the enemy forma-tion. Sometimes the fuse didn't work perfectly, and the cannonball exploded too early or too late to maximise the lethality index. So shrapnel was not at first recognised as the great discovery it was until the trench warfare of World War I. Then it really came into its own, as shrapnel pellets rained down so effectively on trenches and troops in the open. And fuses by then were more reliable. There was still trouble with the height of burst – too high and the pellets scattered over too wide an area – too low and the pellets were less lethal. But during the 1914–17 stalemate there was lots of time for gunners on both sides to perfect their skills, and unlimited ammunition, and shrapnel began to reach its proper projected lethality index.

Now, said Joan Lumb, and this was the point she had been reaching, later in that war, a high explosive shell was developed which also exploded in the air with a timed fuse. It was the pieces of shell which wounded, not the contents of the shell. It was terminologically inexact to refer to wounds made from the shell itself as 'shrapnel wounds', and an insult to Henry Shrapnel. This incorrect usage continued through World War II, and Joan Lumb wished to set the record straight. The press was there tonight, and she hoped it would stand up to its reputation as fair and unbiased, and make this very important point clear to the public.

Mew smiled and nodded. She thought Joan Lumb was mad, but seemed the only one around the table who did.

She asked Panza what a lethality index was. He explained that it was the number of deaths any one weapon could expect to bring about in its lifetime, if properly and effectively used. The index of an Assyrian spear was 23, a crossbow 33, a musket 19, a sixteenth-century cannon 43, a great step forward with the eighteenth-century Gaundeval cannon to 940, a howitzer 657,215—
'That's enough,' said Mew. 'I understand.'
He seemed sorry not to go on.

22

After dinner the guests moved to the big drawing-room, where more coffee and brandy was served. The guests stood and talked, or sat and talked, or moped (Murray) as their natures and circumstances suggested. Have I properly described this room to you? I doubt it: it is so uninteresting. You know what these large reception rooms in country houses are like! They are designed to suit everyone and offend no one, and end up having no identity at all, like a woman with too placatory a nature. The occasional tables are highly polished and upon them stand tall blue and white ceramic vases, vaguely oriental, on which the eye prefers not to linger – though they can sometimes fetch amazing prices at the auction room. The sofas and chairs, grouped uneasily about the room, are slip-covered with chintz (Bella chose to sit in the one exotic armchair the Shrapnel Academy boasted – and that was wonderfully deep and redly velvet), and the rugs on the parquet floors are undistinguished, although there will sometimes be some really pleasant watercolours on the walls. The only remarkable things about the drawing-room of the Shrapnel Academy were the large and striking portrait of the three world leaders at Yalta above the fireplace and, during the course of the evening, the size of the fire in the grate as Joan Lumb tried, and failed, to drive back and out unusual and rather unpleasant cooking smells which kept back-blowing down the chimney.

Joan Lumb pressed the General to give a brief résumé of his forthcoming lecture, and he obliged. His thesis was that World War II, contrary to common belief, had not been a mishmash of events, but had progressed to its ending through a series of decisive battles. He cited in particular the USA field artillery shoot against Kwajalein Island in the Pacific: a relatively small target, 4,500,000 square yards; 65,000 105mm and 155mm shells were laid upon it – that is to say one shell burst for every sixty-nine square yards. Yet 20 per cent of its population survived, only a little hurt or shocked – being in trenches, dugouts or concrete emplacements.

Mew interrupted to ask if this massacre counted as a battle, and the General said in his view yes. The population referred to was for the most part soldiery, and attempting to fight back: that made it definitely a battle. A decisive battle was one in which much was sacrificed, but something of supreme importance saved – whether it was Greek Wisdom, Roman Virtue, Saxon Bravery, French Democracy – or, as at Kwajalein, American World Dominance. If Mew would remain quiet he would deal with these matters in due course. Click! Click! went Mew, when Muffin wasn't looking. '"America seeks world domination," says Nato General.' Click! Click!

The General went on to cite what even he called the Massacre of Dieppe, rather than the Battle of Dieppe. (Sometimes slaughter awes even those who organise it.) But even that had brought about a long-term blessing. The sacrifice had not been in vain. In August 1942 two Canadian brigades attempted an invasion of German–occupied France, at Dieppe. It was, said the General, frankly, a face-saving exercise, a PR junket, to offset the loss of Tobruk. The 2nd Canadian division was simply to sally forth in high summer and disembark on the Dieppe esplanade. Everyone knew the Canadians were legendary fighting men: they'd go in with tanks to muzzle any machine-guns, commandos to disable the flanking batteries. They'd catch the enemy by surprise. But it didn't work. Of 4,963 Canadians who set sail, only 2,110 returned. 'How can you possibly see that as glorious?' asked Mew. Joan Lumb resolved never again to ask anyone to dinner she had not personally met and approved.

Joan Lumb, in her heart, had declared Mew an enemy. Joan Lumb, in fact, lived in much the same frame of mind as Harry the dog, when it came to enemies and non-enemies. Not that Harry was in any particular frame of mind at the time, and never would be, unless theories of reincarnation were true, in which case he was at that very moment being reborn as a lion, if it's valour that counts, or a rather nasty earwig, if friendliness is required for progress on the Great Wheel of Life. He had been taken from the stew-pot, drained, and boned, and was now being pounded into a mixture of oil, egg and spices. If only we knew what it was like to be dead, how much better would we not all run our lives! We would know whose life to spare and whose to take: whether kidney dialysis for the elderly was worth a nation's resources; whether abortion was okay or not; whether euthanasia ought to be condoned by the Church: we would know whether it was better to die young of cold and hunger in Napoleon's Grand Retreat, or to live to fifty and die of TB, looking eighty; we would know whether battles were worth the excitement and amputations worth the pain: we would know whether to give child murderers longer or shorter sentences than bank robbers: we would know whether to be sorry for Harry that he is being pounded up into pâté, or glad for him that he has been spared the murderous passions of his life. But we don't: our after-life does not inform our living. We have to put up with any number of uncertainties. There is no one to tell us: there can be no proof, only this conviction or that, and so, not knowing death, we can never give proper weight to life. We have to muddle along.

The General, unlike Joan Lumb, quite liked the look of Mew, this young woman with her reds and pinks, her strong face, and the smudge of oil beneath her ear. And Bella would keep. She always had in the past. He had forgotten Shirley. With every year that passed he forgot more and more. But then, he had more and more to forget.
'My dear,' he said, 'these are complex matters. A 47 per cent casualty rate? It's high, but who is to say what is *too* high? It's an arbitrary figure. Is a hundred deaths a hundred times worse than one death? I think not. Come and see me afterwards. We'll talk about it. Many of those killed were

French Canadians. Les Fusiliers de Mont-Royal, in particular, during their ten-minute run-in to the French beaches,
were drenched with fire as they touched ground. Over a
hundred men were killed on the spot. Still they came on!
This courage was not wasted. It put the French Canadians
back on the world's map. If Quebec speaks French today,
it is because of the sacrifice – conscious or unknowing – of
those brave men, those gallant commandos.'

Shirley yawned. She thought the commandos sounded
pretty foolish, but knew better than to say so. What would
they have done if they had captured Dieppe, all alone in
1942? She bet no one had worked that out. PR was PR: the
deed in itself enough. She was glad Victor had left the army,
and gone into business instead. She wondered whether she
ought not to go up again and see how the children were –
and then thought perhaps not. Supposing Hilda were still
there? She would have to face her dark reproachful eyes,
and be made to feel like a neglectful mother. She felt she
had been sitting idly for long enough. She wondered if
perhaps she should go and check up on Harry's welfare –
her sister-in-law had been almost as brisk and brutal in
disposing of the dog as she had been in the disposing of the
children. But then she would have to venture downstairs
through the green baize door, and who knew what she might
meet? She had trouble enough encountering a single au-pair
girl in her own kitchen, or a cleaning lady in her own
bathroom; she had the feeling there were hundreds, hundreds down below. And Harry could surely look after himself. And she was not, she admitted, all that fond of Harry,
Peacebarker. A beautiful animal, but sinister; storing up
emotions which it had no means of voicing. Rather, in fact,
like Bella Morthampton, whom Victor now held in rather
intimate conversation. That is to say, Victor talked and
Bella watched the movements his mouth made, as if it was
his mouth rather than his words which interested her.

Shirley resolutely turned her attention from Victor and
Bella, and back to the General. He wanted sympathy;

particularly, it seemed to Shirley, from Mew. He had had to take sleeping pills, he was saying, ever since D-Day plus five, when he'd been obliged to give orders to have a small French hill-top town destroyed, in order to save his advancing troops. What a predicament! The French were allies, there were non-combatants in the town, but there was German artillery as well. Twenty-five thousand of his own men were advancing. A terrible choice! He blew up the town: old men and women, children, allies, and saved his men. The greater, long-term priority was the success of the thrust into Germany.

'These are the dreadful dilemmas a man in my position has to face,' mourned the General. 'I have not had a proper night's sleep for forty years.'

'Bad luck,' said Mew.

And well, yes, of course, so it was. Bad luck for little baby Leo, Colonel and Mrs Makeshift's only son, that he grew up to have this kind of decision forced upon him. That he happened to be where he was, when he was, with just those number of flashes upon his uniform; in such a time and place that all around turned to him and said, 'What shall we do?' and he the one elected to give the answer. How can a man just do nothing in such circumstances? He can't. Perhaps you think young Leo should have refused promotion and stayed a captain? But even captains sometimes have to decide, in time of war, whether this trooper will die or that, though on the whole the fate of whole towns is left to generals (and that of nations mostly to Supreme Commanders; in consultation with the civilian powers, of course – if there's time). And there are only so many hours in one night, and so much sleep a man can lose, so one might as well, in terms of consequence, be hanged for a sheep as well as a lamb, lose a town's population as a single man: have a general's pay and not a captain's. And only the brave deserve the fair, and the fair go to those of highest rank – and when the bells ring out to warn us, or promise us, that peace is over, that war's begun, there's joy among the ranks. Promotion's on the way! Better food, better wine,

123

and a batman to clean your boots! What price insomnia now? Of course the General did not, could not, refuse promotion. Nor would you, had you been him.

What we have to decide, of course, once we've settled the vexing matter of what happens to us after death, is whether it is a hundred times worse to kill a hundred men than it is to kill one man. Do numbers really make much difference? Everyone dies in the end. Killing is merely the cutting short of lives. Is it worse to kill a child than an adult, and if so, why? Is it worse to kill an ally than an enemy, and if so, for whom? If there had been 250 troops approaching, not 25,000, ought the General to have blown up the town? And what if the town had contained a school for crippled children? Would that have made a difference? If one of the children were the infant Jesus? By what criteria did General Leo Makeshift proceed? Did he use reason, or sentiment, or what?

But that was in a war long gone, and a war comparatively merciful, at least for those engaged in it. The engagement casualties per day (for the USA) ran at 0.9 per division. In World War I the figure was 20 per cent, and back a little further in the American Civil War, it was as high (at least for the Confederate troops) as 28.9 per cent. The fact is that the army (this side or that) is getting much better at looking after its own. In the Lethality Indices a one-megaton nuclear air burst is reckoned at 695,385,000, and you needn't lose a single one of your own men. Sorry! I did say I wouldn't lapse into these plaintive civilian whines. Let's get on with the story.

'Bad luck,' said Mew. So it was. Downstairs, though the mass of Harry himself had been removed from the pot, the stock continued to simmer – cumin and ginger and dog-ear and dog-brain – and to send its aromas through the Shrapnel Academy.

Shirley wondered whether to go over and join Victor and

Bella, but pride forbade it. Victor, she told herself, was being just ordinarily charming, as all top executives learn to be. Smooth, smooth! Stroke, stroke! Interested in everyone, everything, fair, reasonable, even with a joke or two, though these do have to be rather carefully learned by heart. But a sense of humour oils the sometimes choppy waters of industry; so all executives have one. Shirley stood alone and a little forlornly in her flowered dress and wondered if she should try and talk to Murray, who sat, apparently in isolation equal to her own, puffing his pipe, tapping his heavy-booted foot, staring into the fire, as if he were not in a civilised drawing-room at all, but in some jungle clearing surrounded by mosquitoes. He said something, to no one in particular.

'What did you say?' asked Shirley.

'Funny smell,' he repeated. 'Smelt something like it once before – can't quite put my finger on it.'

Shirley looked at the forefinger he held up. Instead of finishing with a nail, it was tipped with a long corrugated scar. She shuddered.

Outside, snow continued to fall.

23

Bad deeds escalate: even little ones. They get tossed like a magic ball between one human being and another, back and forth, getting bigger every time: you did *this* so I'll do *that*, until the hands cannot hold it, the burden is too great: and the ball falls, and bursts, and turns out to be full of some kind of murderous corrosive acid which, once it begins to flow, cannot be stopped; a whole river of malice, burning, maiming, killing as it goes, and widows, and widowers too these days, and orphans weep every time a wrong is righted, and people hop around the street blinded or one-legged, and then the flow of malice slows to a trickle, and stops and dries up, like the chain reaction from the first atomic bombs over New Mexico. It's finished. The ball's empty. But terrible until it is. So never say a harsh word if you can say a kind one: it may be you who starts the war.

'Dirty Catholic!' you say, or 'stupid Irish' or 'I hate all Americans' or 'pinko Commies'. Don't! Don't! Or, 'She shrunk my sweatshirt so I'll stay out all night' or 'He crashed my car so I'll phone his wife'. Don't! Stop it! Click, click! 'Car Bomb Massacre – 40 dead', 'Broken-home child in suicide bid!', 'Wife and lover in Deep Freeze Horror!' 'Terrorist dies in police station leap.'

If Muffin had not told Joan Lumb about Mew's photographs, everything might have been different.

If Murray had been more responsive to Joan Lumb, who loved and admired him above all men, excepting only Henry Shrapnel, and he was dead, everything would have been different. (Joan Lumb avoided Murray after dinner. She was hurt because her company did not seem to make him happy, as his did her.)

If Shirley had not been such an easy prey to the prejudices and illusions of her time, and vain about her hands, and upset by the close attention Victor was paying to Bella—

If Victor had been more courteous: if Bella had recognised the existence of other women—

But Muffin, Murray, Joan Lumb, Victor, Shirley, Bella were the product of their times, as their parents had been before them, and the times move inexorably on from one recorded event to another, from Tiglath-Pileser to the man on the moon, and the times are too strong for them. How can anyone, Joan Lumb, Baf, the General, Hilda, Edna (remember her, the taxi driver?) stop scrambling up the slopes and turn and outface this frightful tidal wave of destiny? But it has to be done. It is all we can do. We are better, braver swimmers than we think.

Now.

Throughout the evening the staff had been gathering in the kitchens to celebrate and/or lament the passing and pulverising of Harry. Brown eyes clustered and gleamed in the dim light. (Joan Lumb insisted on low-wattage bulbs in the staff quarters. It was one of the economies of which she was most proud.) More and more came until finally there seemed to be a shifting yet solid wall ringing the cooking pot and chopping board, mostly coloured Muslim black and grey, patched by the blue of the worshippers of Mao and lightened by the occasional glimmer of Hindu silk. As the jigsaw surface changed and moved, gaps in the wall would appear, through which the occasional child would thrust a bare arm or leg, having successfully burrowed to the front, the better to be near the pot and the block, to catch the smell of the fall of the great, the humiliation of the oppressor. A susurration drifted up, along with the rank odour of Harry and the sweet lingering smell that badly boiled pumpkin and overcooked fish leave behind; it was composed of the murmurs and prayers of the old, and the low chattering of the young, and the sharp intakes of breath of the frightened and the soft ululations of the distressed, quickly hushed. This, all understood, was a moment of destiny. Nothing could be the same again.

Acorn stood upon a table to address the crowd. Silence fell; only Miriam's baby, held in Matilda's arms, lamented at the back of the room and wouldn't be hushed. (Matilda had to go out with it.) Acorn spoke in English: his voice had gained that arrogant edge of the leader into violence: it is the voice of those who give permission to hate: who enlist God on the devil's side. It is jagged edged: into it fit, with the greatest ease, the matching jagged-edges of anger, misery, spite, paranoia, self-pity, fear and loathing of every kind: it is Henry Shrapnel's exploding cannonball put together again: and put together it appears as a nice round ball of self-righteousness.

'We are the Family of the Unknown,' cries Acorn to the crowd. 'We are the People of Now. We are everywhere, yet we are nowhere. We are the brown, the black, the helpless hands which serve and are not seen.'
Reader, it is true. The hands that serve you, in any corner of the world, are mostly female, and usually brown, and for the most part go unnoticed; or stay anonymous. Who cleans your offices? Do you know? No. You'd rather not. Who stands in the steam to press your shirt: who cut the upper of your fashion boot? The Family of the Unknown, that's who. The Myriad People of Now: the scuttling, scurrying, frightened, passive people of the earth, the dusters of cannon, the polishers of buttons. No wonder the staff listened now to Acorn.

Run the cannonball down a snowy slope; see it collecting snow, collecting support, getting bigger and bigger as it runs: the shrapnel of rage and right encased deep but certain below: oh, they were all ears! Who wouldn't be, and the scent of Harry inflamed their senses with the notion that action is possible, revolutions happen, things *change*: and how handsome Acorn was: personable, powerful, frightening, but unfrightened. Pin your colours to that mast: oh yes, it is the only mast you have, and anyway, if you don't it'll only fall on you and crush you.

'Brothers, sisters,' said Acorn, and who could not want to be included in this family? 'We will live no longer under the yoke of oppression; we will strike back: we will wipe out the transgressors against God. We have nothing to fear but fear itself.'
A few faces looked puzzled. It seemed to them that there was a great deal to fear: homelessness, hunger, cold, prison, death.
'Miriam is dead,' said Acorn, in his new gritty, shrapnelly voice. 'Murdered! A life for a life; a dozen of theirs must equal one of ours. Say to yourself, brothers, sisters, who harms my brother, my sister, in the Family of the Unknown, harms me. And vengeance must be ours!'

And if there were those who thought, well: it could be said equally that Acorn's baby murdered its mother; or that Acorn's refusal to let the medical services in hadn't helped: or that Acorn's sequestration of the meat money hadn't helped Miriam's health, no one said so. That Joan Lumb's action in overlooking the formalities of visas and so forth might be construed as kindness (albeit mixed with self-interest) rather than simple exploitation went unremarked upon.
'Brothers, sisters,' said Acorn from his soap-box table, and his eyes rolled and his clenched fist struck into the heavy air, 'death is nothing. Better we are all dead than live with shame another day!'

There came a slight harrumphing from the front. Inverness disengaged himself from the human jigsaw of the wall and sat upon the edge of the table, legs swinging, spectacles glinting. He seemed a very modest, small, elderly man, sitting thus at Acorn's feet. Acorn's legs were vast and tall above, like shiny pillars. Inverness smiled, in a situation and position where smiling seemed unthinkable. And, even as he smiled, he undermined Acorn's case. Many trembled for Inverness's sake. He would follow Harry into the pot if he wasn't careful – or bits of him, which he'd then be obliged to eat, and probably not in sandwich form.

'But what is our objective?' asked Inverness, innocently, his head turned up towards Acorn. 'What can be gained by violence? I have seen too much of it. So have most of us who make our refuge here. I quite agree: there must be change. But let us be reasonable, let us negotiate. Let us present our complaints in the proper way.'

'You are a fool,' said Acorn, but it was a mistake on his part to so much as acknowledge Inverness's presence. Eyes turned to the older man's face, and the slight, sad smile. Inverness had patched cuts, and delivered babies, and cured pain, and counselled patience and acceptance. And his courage was immense: he was a fish nibbling where the shark thought he oughtn't.

'I may be a fool,' said Inverness, 'but better a live fool than a dead hero.'

'There are the words of a coward,' said Acorn, 'and a traitor to the Family of the Unknown, the People of Now.'

'We are warm, we are fed, we are safe,' said Inverness, leaving his perch upon the table rather suddenly, and returning to stand in front of the people's wall, as if making himself their spokesman. 'What more do we want?'

'Dignity,' said Acorn. 'Justice. Vengeance. Blood.'

'I would rather have a hot dinner any day,' said Inverness, and around him people laughed.

'This is no man! This is a woman who speaks,' sneered Acorn, and the laughing quickly stopped. He pressed home his advantage. 'This is a man who killed our sister by his neglect,' said Acorn. 'He is in the pay of our oppressors: he is a spy: he speaks for them, and not for you. He drips his words like poison. Shut your ears to them, my brothers and sisters, before they deafen you to the truth. Lo, the fruit of our hatred—'

And he held above his head the silver tray where the spirit of Harry rested, trapped between two slivers of bread, and a breath of wonder welled up like a current of air hot enough and strong enough to take the weight of the tray, so that it seemed to support itself, and not need Acorn's hands at all, but just to float there. A miracle! Or was it a trick of the light?

'The dog is dead!' cried Acorn, 'and yet it lives! Today they killed one of us and didn't know it. Today they shall eat the dog and not know that.'

'And what then?' asked Inverness; though now elbows and shoulders obstructed him, tried to ease him away from the front of the crowd. 'Detail, please. Detail!'

'Then we will kill them,' shrieked Acorn. 'We will boil them alive.'

'And what happens to us then?' persisted Inverness, now from the depths of the crowd. 'When the snow melts and the authorities arrive? When our crime is disclosed? What do we say? Perhaps that the entire dinner party was spirited away by flying saucers?'

'Still piping away, woman?' asked Acorn, dancing up and down with rage. 'Careful, or I'll tear your voice out of your woman's throat! See these hands? They will crush the breath from the enemies of the People of Now. They will tear the flesh off the bones of our enemies. There will be a risotto: the most wonderful risotto the world has ever known. For once there will be no shortage of meat. We will eat the dinner party!'

Reader, you may think all this too crude, too simple, but have you listened to the Watergate Tapes? It is hard to imagine how barbarous the language of our leaders is, in private, how simple and emotive their judgements, how their love of money and power and vengeance rises to the surface like the white crust on boiling strawberry jam. They know no better than you or me; they behave a good deal worse. And how gullible we are, so long as it suits us! Oh, *Nixon*, you say! Nixon was an exception. *Really?* What about Gaddafi: how many children have been blown to bits since he made his first 'sweep them into the sea' speech twenty years ago? Since he first gave permission to hate? How many have died so the Basques can be free? Free from what? The Common Market? Oh, terror! Discover outrage, and a few good phrases, promise pain now and justice later, vengeance for past affronts and any Leader of Man's away. If you belonged to the Family of the Unknown, the People of Now, what would you do? Fight back? Eat the dinner party? You bet! So would I. Can you imagine anything more tedious than Inverness's proposed proper presentation of complaints? Acorn's right. We *don't* want him in the Family.

To get back to the matter of the possible eating of the dinner party, I find the very idea disconcerting, the more I consider it, and the idea is mine, so it may disconcert you, reader, even more. But in the scale of human depravity, is such a deed particularly bad? Victor, that very day, that equable family man, and though indirectly, had been the cause of several deaths by malnutrition in southern India. that is to say, they would not have died had Chewinox not pulled out of the area. The handsome and virile General, as we know, had many thousands of deaths to his credit and could happily contemplate more. Lovely Baf was a dealer in death and pain. Panza and Sergei sent weariness and depression abroad; fed it into the hearts of the young. Murray killed with his bare hands. If death deserves death, then surely they deserved to die? And all, what is more, killed those who had never offended them. Now Acorn was personally upset, affronted and damaged by the behaviour of Upstairs, and yet his reaction, to kill, cook and eat, and thus incorporate and control the evil, seems to us on the instant far more reprehensible than anything perpetrated by his putative victims. At any rate it does to me.

24

Remember Mew's motorbike? The one she abandoned so
blithely at the side of the road when it ran out of petrol? It
was not her bike, in fact, but belonged to a boy named
Terry, which was perhaps why she forgot it so easily. It was
a Harley-Davidson, a collector's piece, circa 1952, not that
that meant anything much to Mew, who was the kind of
person who far prefers the present to the past and was just
as happy with a plastic spoon as a silver one. Whatever
Mew did with his Harley-Davidson – took it, crashed it,
lost it, left it in a country lane in a snowstorm, sold it – was
okay by Terry, so hopelessly did he love Mew. She, for her
part, despised and neglected Terry, but his unrequited
passion did give her a nice kind of confidence. It is always
pleasant to have someone around, of either sex, to love you
no matter what you do, or with whom. Perhaps it was that
Terry was sending thought waves out to Mew, over the
aether – as the Edwardians used to call it – at any rate Mew
remembered his bike and went over to Muffin, interrupting
her conversation with Sergei. That is to say, Sergei was
talking and Muffin was doing her best to listen.
'Of course,' said Sergei, 'orthodox historians merely say the
library burned, that 400,000 rolls were lost, but there's no
real evidence about where the fire started, or how. There's
a scholarly account of what happened in P. M. Fraser's
Ptolemaic Alexandria but who's to say he didn't make the
whole thing up? Trust, these days, is such a difficult thing!'
Muffin wasn't even listening. She kept her eyes on his face
and nodded and looked interested, but it did not deceive
him. He had had many students like that, over the years,
who had acquired the art of paying attention and blanking
off. His voice faded away. He was discouraged. Once he
had commanded the interest of millions of television viewers:

they had stopped him in the street to shake his hand: shop assistants nudged one another when he entered their premises – now no one knew, or cared, or listened. And what did the future hold, except the increasing inattention of listeners, as he grew older, less in command of himself and the world, and so less worth listening to?

Muffin too had a pain in her heart. Bella sat languidly in the dark red velvet armchair, one thin pale arm, palm upward, held across the folds of her black dress, almost as if waiting for an injection, some kind of fix: and on one solid arm of the chair perched Victor, and on the other Baf. Bella, Muffin noticed, hardly ever spoke at all. Men spoke to her. It had taken Muffin some time to realise that the pain in her heart was not indigestion from the caribou patties, but a mixture of jealousy and grief.

'Muffin,' said Mew, and both Sergei and Muffin were glad to be diverted from their thoughts, 'I've just remembered something. I dumped my bike by the side of the road. I ought to do something about it. It isn't even my bike.'

Muffin went to the tall windows and parted the curtains a little and looked outside, over the white landscape. The wind had dropped, and the light from the windows sent its brilliance curiously far out into the night, as if the snow itself was a source of light. The trees were out of proportion: even the very tall ones started out of the ground half-way up their trunks and the short ones seemed to have no trunks at all, merely hydrocephalic heads. Funny, thought Muffin. 'It really has been snowing!' she said. 'I don't suppose anything can be done tonight. But we'll send a Land-Rover out to pick it up tomorrow morning. Why didn't you say something earlier?'
'Forgot,' said Mew. And so she had. 'Well,' she said now, 'I don't suppose it'll rust or anything,' and moved away, her duty to Terry done. One must at least show an interest, when faced with the problems of borrowed property. So much her mother had taught her, in her saner moments.

Muffin was accustomed to cities, where snow melts almost as it falls, in the warmth of a million exhalations, a million footfalls. But Sergei knew his Nature better. He looked out over Muffin's shoulder, and said:

'There isn't a hope in hell of getting anything moving out there before a thaw, and that's not going to be soon. You realise what it means? There'll be no lecture tomorrow.'

'You tell Joan,' said Muffin, pouting. 'I'm not going to.'

'You look very pretty when you do that,' said Sergei. 'Do it again!'

She did, and felt better. It is, as I say, always nice to be admired. And Sergei was gratified by her response to his flattery, if not to the information he had to offer. How quickly we shift from dull despair to animation, given the right circumstances. Men should always admire women and women men, or seem to. It can do no one any harm and improves the general atmosphere no end.

'I'm not going to tell Joan,' said Sergei. 'Let her find out for herself. It doesn't do round here to be the bearer of bad news.'

The guests helped themselves to brandy and coffee. The absence of the staff went unobserved. Only Mew noticed and regretted the loss of Acorn, whose buttocks under black silk so entranced her. But perhaps, later that night, he would reappear? He knew, after all, which her room was. Perhaps, under the shadow of Trident rising from the sea, black and white could mix and mingle, and click! click! 'Black Butler Tells All! Wealth Above, Poverty Below!' 'Darling, darling, tell me all, even as you show me how you love me.' Click! Click! 'Let me remember, when all this is over, the words, and not the occasion. Let me be right. Let me be justified. Let the pursuit of truth be worth the betrayal of love—'

But now the General was crossing to talk to Mew. His face was ravaged with deep lines: she found that not repellent but attractive. His hair, though snowy-white, was thick. A bird in the hand, however scraggy, is worth two in the bush, where sexual matters are concerned. All the same, Mew wondered at the catholic, and indeed the heterosexual nature of her inclinations, which could so happily and swiftly include both the young black man and the old white man as objects of desire. And why was she not moved at all by Muffin, in spite of her long legs and high buttocks? Perhaps it was just the feel of Muffin's silk skirt around her legs – an unfamiliar sensation; usually there was just the brisk rub of denim – or was it the shoes, now she was accustomed to them, which made her feel oddly and agreeably heterosexual? Or perhaps she'd just had too much to drink: or perhaps it was all the talk of war, and the feeling that you'd better now, or tomorrow you might be dead. The prospect of eternal peace, eternal silence, is a great aphrodisiac.

'Tell me, General,' said Mew briskly, 'how the lethality indices for weapons correlates with the mortality rates of troops in the field?'

'As one goes up,' said the General, 'the other goes down. That is how, in the army, we reckon progress.'

'So progress in the military sense,' observed Mew, 'means more and more civilians killed.'

'More and more civilians killed *potentially*,' said the General. 'Of course in wartime soldiers are a great deal more valuable than civilians. But these aren't matters a pretty girl should worry about; especially not at a party. If you seriously want to interview me, what's wrong with midnight in the library?'

'Nothing,' said Mew, which still left her free for Acorn under Trident later. The library today, Trident tomorrow! 'Good heavens,' thought Mew, 'if this is drunk let me have more of it.'

Baf went upstairs to his room in the new wing. Above the door were the words *Mother Teresa*. The unusual naming of the room was Joan Lumb's idea.

'Are you sure?' Muffin had asked.

'Of course I'm sure,' said Joan Lumb.

'But the students might find it embarrassing,' said Muffin. 'Fancy having to say to someone who's in Julius Caesar, oh, I'm in Mother Teresa!'

136

'It is important for them to learn,' said Joan Lumb, 'that the army *cares.*'

Of course, everyone knows about Mother Teresa. Unsupported by any government agency, and only by private funds, Mother Teresa runs a hospice for the dying poor of Calcutta. She gathers the wretched off the streets so they can die, as they have not lived, in an atmosphere of love. She has room for some 2,000. If, in Bombay, on the other side of that crowded continent, you remark upon the number of dead, dying and starving in the streets, you are, as likely as not, to be told, it's all right, Mother Teresa looks after them. Mother Teresa is a household name the world over; of course she is, of course you know about her: she is the one who cares so we need not. Joan Lumb admires her very much, and she is admirable. Muffin thought Joan Lumb had put Baf in Mother Teresa to annoy her, and was right. She had. Fortunately Baf didn't even notice the words above the door.

In the wall above the fireplace of Mother Teresa was a safe. It was hidden behind a rather pleasant Victorian print of Jesus driving the money-lenders from the Temple, especially selected for the room by Joan Lumb. Baf got the key from Muffin before dinner and, before going downstairs, he'd locked his Victorian knife box safely inside. The value of the contents ran into many millions. Sometimes Baf marvelled that he, so young, had so much responsibility upon his shoulders. But this was the age of the young. Baf had failed many examinations at school, but had always charmed both teachers and pupils. Since his school was of the expensive English kind, which has grounds spacious enough to house bodyguards as well as pupils, he made the acquaintance there of the sons of the intolerably rich and intolerably powerful of all nations. He became, over the summer holidays, acquainted with the insides of palaces and embassies everywhere. There was no point in him staying at home. It was his mother's custom to spend the months between June and October either in a religious retreat or in a nursing home for alcoholics.

Now Baf carefully lifted out the knife box from its home behind the print of Jesus and the money-lenders, laid it on his bedside table, and opened it, as much to admire its contents as to make sure it was as he had left it. How neatly the tiny, steely, intricate objects lay in their soft velvet home. They were beautiful: made in metals that entranced the eye, being so like and yet unlike the familiar substances of everyday life. There was no overt decoration: there was no need: the three-dimensional fractals (pyramids within pyramids, globes within globes) of which these slivers of weapons must of necessity be composed if they were to have the strength required of them, created surfaces which seemed to live, and quiver, and change, although the mind knew well enough that they did not. But the eye is used to what it is used to, and sees what it is in the habit of seeing; and an effort of will must sometimes be made if it is to register fact, not fiction: just as the staff below, even as Baf took out his knife box and opened it on the marvels within, looked en masse at the silver tray above Acorn's head and thought it floated.

'How foolish those people are,' thought Baf, 'who believe that money is man's prime motivation!' Baf got 12 per cent of every weapon sold, and was a millionaire many times over – though it would have been most imprudent of him to live according to his means – but this, of course, was not why he promoted and sold the weapons. Man is not so base as you might think. Baf was proud of his products, and of the ingenuity and skill which had gone into their devising, and of the beauty of the objects themselves, and he wanted them to be used because he wanted them proved; and whole armies to be proud of them, and rely on them, just as Baf himself did. The money was a symbol of all these things: a testimonial to his professionalism, not an end in itself. (Mind you, it is easy enough for a millionaire to take this rather high view of money.)

So Baf took the knife box out not so much because he wanted to persuade the General to persuade his Ministry to purchase the weapons, as because he was proud of them, and wanted to show them to the General, and for the General to say, 'Hey, that's great!' Just as staff generals want to show the President the missiles rising like silver wands from their silos, and hear him say 'Fellers, that's great! Most impressive!' We all want our father's admiration and, if we don't get it, spend our lives looking for it. What's the betting Baf's father was a hard guy to please? I'm telling you, very hard. That's why his wife, Baf's mother, took to drink and religious mania. But that's another story. Baf went back downstairs, took the General to a far corner of the room and opened the knife box. Joan Lumb fortunately did not notice, or no doubt would have cried 'Security' and demanded that he close it at once.

The General admired in particular the cylinder, rather like a latticed cigarette-lighter, whose tiny facets caught the whole light range of colour, so it seemed to live inside its own rainbow. This cylinder contained, under enormous pressure, enough new improved CS gas to subdue the entire audience at the Rose Bowl, and leave not a single child nor babe in arms not coughing, spluttering, gasping and weeping. It could of course be simply converted to the containment of more lethal nerve gases, but Baf found himself neurotic about these, and given a choice – which he was, his employers being civilised and kindly people – had gone for the least effective of all the martial gases. He apologised to the General for what might be seen as a lack of conviction on his part.

'That's okay by me,' said the General, who was eyeing Mew in preparation for his midnight interview with her in the library, and was rather pleased to see that she had unshaven legs. He suspected that denoted passion, that she would not be finickity. He could not abide reluctant women, who had to be stroked, and prodded, and persuaded. Life was too short.

'I can see you wouldn't want to carry the really nasty stuff

about. Not in a box like that. Where's the shielding? Where's
the protection?'

Baf was able to explain to the General that the great
advantage of miniaturised weapons was the comparative
ease and safety of their deployment. The velvet-lined knife
box was to the Minitox Range as a lead-lined concrete
bunker to any conventional cylinder of toxic gas. The knife
box, moreover, was not quite so simple as it seemed. Beneath
the vellum surface was a vacuum layer, maintained by a
minute vacuum pump, battery-powered, which kept the
contents still: bounce it about as Baf might – 'don't,' said
the General – the weapons stayed quiet in their alcoves. Baf
drew the General's attention to one of his favourites: the
pencil napalm-thrower, which could incinerate a whole
platoon from a hundred yards and they would never know
what happened to them. Another advantage of the miniaturised range was that men were spared the anticipation of
death. This could only be good for their morale. 'Um,' said
the General. But he admired the object. Being made up of
globes within globes, from crystals grown bio-chemically, it
radiated a steady white aura.
'Isn't that radioactive?' he asked, and then apologised. 'I'm
not as young as I was. I'm used to thinking things that glow
are either radioactive or magic.' He went on to explain to
Baf that while miniaturised cannons and guns, both for shot
and gas, missiles and flame throwers, would indeed change
the face of conventional warfare, the point was, could anyone
these days afford the change! Difficult for a modern state to
behave like the Assyrians and live off booty: the money had
to come from somewhere!

Baf said he'd been trying the home market first, naturally,
but would presently have to sell abroad. The investment in
research and development had been enormous. The General
said that was Baf's problem, not his. He, the General, was
most interested in the weapons and had much enjoyed
seeing them but he had given Baf names at the Ministry

and what more could he do? The General was beginning to sound cross.

The General smiled at Mew, who smiled back and wondered what it was that Baf was showing the General.
Click, click, went Mew's camera, produced from up her sleeve, in the general direction of Baf's open knife box. She'd finished the film. The faintest click told her so.

'What does Baf *do*?' asked Mew of Muffin. Stuck away as she had been at the end of the dinner table, she had had no opportunity to discover where, as it were, he was at. But she suspected him of something underhand. His smile was too bright, his face too boyish, as he turned it trustingly towards the General.
'He's some kind of international salesman,' said Muffin, vaguely.
'Don't you *know*? Aren't you his girlfriend?'
'I was,' said Muffin, sadly, and wondered whether it was really worth her time chatting up Sergei, who had dug his chin so firmly into her shoulder as they stood together looking out into the snow, and so make Baf jealous. But perhaps Baf wouldn't even notice, and it never did to make complications at work. Even as she decided that she and Sergei would be the exception to this latter rule, Baf deserted the arm of Bella's chair.
'What's the matter, glumface?' he hissed into Muffin's ear, and she felt better at once. All the odd pains, in her heart, in her throat, in her mouth, quite disappeared.
'Bella the Bitch is so Boring you wouldn't Believe it,' said Baf, who seemed to feel the need to make amends. 'What a lot of B's! Do you think if we went upstairs anyone would notice?' Muffin said probably, not that she cared. Baf said neither did he care, except about her, Muffin, and they began to make their way towards the door. Baf carried the knife box with him, taking rather especial care of it, as Mew observed. What, she wondered, was in it? What interested the General so? Would it be worth seducing Baf, over the weekend, the better to steal it? There would be a scoop for

the *Woman's Times*. Her job would be secure: she might even manage private psychiatric treatment for her mother. Beyond and above that, of course, was her public duty. Things went on in the male world of the Shrapnel Academy women ought to know about. If she stole the box, of course, she would have to leave the motorbike in order to make a quick get away. She saw that snow might really get to be a nuisance: great lumps of white stuff standing between you and your ambition. And where was she? Miles from anywhere, cut off from civilisation, with a group of mad people who believed they were sane – pretty much as her mother had done. Mew's mother, tangled in her mind, had one day poured boiling water from the kettle over her daughter's body as she slept. Her father's name was Jason. Mew's mother felt obliged to boil her children, serve them in a stew, as Medea had done. Yet her mother loved her. Mew had not taken offence: it was others who had carted her mother off. But Mew knew disasters happened, when people who believed they were sane, were not, and tangled in their minds.

She thought she should be on the safe side, and sat down on a sofa by which, on a highly polished table, stood a large pot containing an aspidistra plant. The plant was flourishing – the soil, as it should be when growing aspidistras, was all but dry. (The knack of growing good aspidistras is to drench them thoroughly but only occasionally, and always to keep the leaves well dusted. They like to be pot-bound. Don't even dream of re-potting!) It was an easy enough matter to make a little hole in the earth with a casual forefinger, then slip the camera from her sleeve into the hole, and cover it again. Then she rose and stood and stared casually at the painting above the marble fireplace, and tried to feel safe, and failed.

Reader, one would be hard put to it to say whether or not there is such a thing as telepathy. I can report my own experience, and convincingly, but what good to you is my sample of one? I am certainly as ready to believe in the paranormal as I am to believe we all live and die on a lump of rock, a mere 7,926 miles in diameter, whirling and thrumming through infinite space. That notion seems to me the real bummer. Well, there's my own position declared. Yours must be your own. But if Mew felt nervous she was right to be. After all, downstairs serving dishes floated in the air (or were believed to) and the matter of cooking and eating her was under quite serious discussion. The portrait above the mantelpiece did nothing to reassure Mew as to the sanity of man. It was of President Roosevelt, Supremo Stalin and Prime Minister Churchill signing the Yalta Treaty in 1945. Now the Yalta Treaty was the one in which the two great powers – with the third power to make it seem less like a carve-up – did just that: carved up. They divided the world into spheres of influence, without any reference whatsoever to its inhabitants. You take Bulgaria, I'll have Chile. What about Afghanistan? Oh, um, well we'll have that and you take Finland. We absolutely have to have Australia but you can have Korea! And so on. It was at this painting that Mew happened to be staring, having just buried her camera beside the aspidistra, when Acorn and Inverness brought up the good-night cocoa and sandwiches.

Firelight made Mr Gromyko's face – he stood at Stalin's right hand, an agreeable, shrewd young man – dance and smile. He knew what he knew – and still does – that nothing the human mind can conceive won't in time be done. The Family of Now will be with us any minute, killing, looting, raping, holding hostage, disturbing our Sunday lunch. Click! Click! 'Holocaust on Honduras Airfield', 'Model raped in laser space drama', 'Powers split the world in two'. You invent it, they'll do it.
Cocoa was served to the guests. It was poured by Acorn, very civilly, from a silver jug into those rather awkward but ubiquitous thick French cups with angled sides. They were deep green, gold-rimmed. The guests did their best to be at ease with them, but when Acorn handed round a silver tray on which were placed, on beds of lettuce (Israeli), and cress (South African), little soft white sandwiches, filled with a thick and delicious, though slightly strandy, meat pâté, they

were pleased to set down their cups and accept the food. All ate with relish.

Murmurs of appreciation were heard all round.

'Delicious!'

'Wicked!'

'How tasty!'

'But what *is* it?'

Joan Lumb assumed the sandwiches were filled with the remains of the caribou patties, mashed and moulded, and was glad. She hated to see waste. In the morning she would congratulate Acorn. Where was Acorn? She rang for him. Why had he disappeared? The silver tray, with nearly all of the sandwiches gone, and with Sergei now finishing up the lettuce and cress, lay abandoned on the Georgian sidetable. She looked around the room. There were no servants at all in sight, only plenty of large cups of half-finished cocoa, grim and dark-grained around their golden rims. Annoyed, she rang for Acorn again. Nothing happened.

'Murray,' she said, 'I'm getting no reply from the servants' hall. Why do you think that is?'

'You'd better ask your communications expert,' said Murray. 'I'm more of a field-man myself. What's in the sandwiches? Reminds me of something. Can't think what.'

And he ruminated, trying to dislodge strands of meat from between his cracked, yellow, tough teeth.

'Well,' he said gloomily, 'if it is dog I'll know soon enough.'

'Don't be such an old Eeyore, Murray,' chided Joan Lumb. Elsie Blade, her and Victor's mother, had read and re-read *The House at Pooh Corner* to her children. Joan Lumb thought of her mother with sudden and unusual gratitude and smiled at her brother. He smiled back and crossed over to her.

'Tell me,' he said, 'I can't quite remember. Did mother really once make me re-eat a fried egg I had vomited up?'

'Of course,' said Joan Lumb, and lied for her brother's sake, and indeed for her mother's too. They had been strictly brought up, in their own interests, but not, she felt, strictly enough. She herself had finished up everything, always,

dutifully, the slimiest of porridge, the sourest of fish. Victor
had got away with murder, in Joan Lumb's eyes. Nursery
food had to be finished, come what may. It was training for
life. She would be as strict, she knew, with her own children.
By disliking them, by refusing to conceive them, she did
them a favour. Joan Lumb is not all bad. No one is.

Joan Lumb crossed to the window and looked out. Virgin
snow lay smooth and heavy across the landscape. It was
impossible to see where the drive stopped and the lawns
began. The grizzled god Mars, who, in the act of piercing
a beardless youth with a heavy sword, formed the centre-
piece of the ornamental fountain, had lost stomach, thighs,
legs, feet; only the muscle of his fine torso, his powerful
arms, gleamed distantly in the light which Joan Lumb
released from the parted curtains. The snow had stopped
again, and the wind had dropped. Joan Lumb did not like
what she saw, not at all.

'It's too bad,' she said to Murray. 'What are the servants
playing at? They've made no attempt to clear the snow.
Tomorrow's guests will have trouble parking! Not that
they'll let a little weather deter them! But are the servants
deaf and blind? I've rung and rung and nothing happens.'

But Murray took no notice. He was paying attention to
Bella. She was explaining that she ate all the meat she could.
She suffered badly from anaemia. The doctor had said the
best thing for her was raw ox-blood, but she could not
face it. And Murray was telling Bella how once, lost in
Venezuela, he had kept alive by slicing steaks off living
cows. They were getting on like a house on fire. Joan Lumb's
voice faded away. She was unhappy, and not in the habit
of being so. She was quite accustomed to feeling angry, or
irritated, or bored, or resentful, or self-righteous, but not
simply unhappy. Colonel Lumb had never made her unhappy. Her mother, on the other hand, had. 'It's love,' she
thought, 'love makes you unhappy,' and there and then set

145

her heart against Murray. Some women, poor things, have this capacity: to stop loving when it hurts.

Victor finished his first sandwich and Shirley her second and Victor said, 'You'll get fat,' but he might have said 'fatter' and Shirley was grateful for small mercies. Her husband was back at her side, and she felt calm, and relieved, and a little too bright, like a sunny dawn after a stormy night. And Victor was indeed still lingering in that state of marital disaffection which the presence of a deathly glamorous woman can produce in the mildest and most devoted of married men. (Married women do not seem to be quite so disturbed by the presence of beautiful, available and desirable men, but this may be merely custom and convention, and no doubt in the perfect world we all work towards, when unfair gender distinctions have faded away, men and women will be equal in this too.)

Do you want to know, as Shirley longs to, what Victor had said to Bella, as she sat, or rather lounged, stretched, with her long body pressed somehow hard and heavy into the dark red velvet, as if a man's body was already upon her, and the only doubt which one of the men in the room it could possibly be?
Victor had said:
'Bella, from what you say, your work at the Ministry of Defence hardly gives you the opportunities and rewards a young woman of your intelligence and competence should have. Had you ever thought of working in the private sector? In Industry?'
'Can't say I had,' said Bella.
'I think you should seriously consider it,' Victor said. 'Here, let me give you my card. I want you to ring me at this number – see, here's my extension –' and he took her long pale forefinger, with the rather square and flattened nails, and it was cool and smooth to the touch, and he was conscious of the reddened, tough, male hairiness of his hand, so that both fingers, his and hers, pointed to the number –

'and we'll make an appointment, and you will come to visit me at my office and we'll discuss it.'

But Bella took her hand away from Victor's.

'I'm doing okay where I am,' she said, and looked at him and smirked, as if saying 'men! all the same!' and the dream blinked into a nightmare. Her voice had seemed suddenly hard and guttural and quite frightened him. She was a ravenous woman: she would swallow him up, engulf him as she had engulfed her food at dinner. The smirk was possibly because, invisible at her elbow, flapping unseen wings, was a host of sinewy vampires with heavy claws and bloody beaks, which were about to tear him to shreds. That was when he rose and returned to Shirley, his wife. And Shirley had said:

'*Do* have a sandwich, Victor. Keep me company!'

So he did. But still he looked over towards Bella, chatting to Murray. Perhaps the vampires could be outfaced, or even ruled: perhaps to be King of the Vampires was a loftier aim than to be Prince at Gloabal? It was obviously late: he was not thinking sensibly. He said to Shirley:

'Shall we turn in soon?' and she said yes, and smiled at him with simple and endearing wifeliness. Shirley was happy. They would make love: they always did when they were away: a different bed, a different ceiling, the distance of the children, those reminders of ordinariness, permanence, refreshed the pleasure. He would try not to think of Bella; it was a discourtesy to Shirley.

'Okay?' he asked again, and again she said yes, and he rubbed her warm cheek with the same hand that had lately touched Bella. He supposed Bella would presently rejoin the General, but the General was rather surprisingly deep in conversation with the young woman journalist with the dirty face. 'I can't think why Joan asked her,' he complained to Shirley. 'She's obviously the kind to make trouble.'

'I wondered myself,' said Shirley, taking another bite of sandwich. 'But I think she's *you-know*.' She meant lesbian. Victor was astonished. Was Shirley implying that his sister had homosexual inclinations? He asked as much.

'But, Victor,' said Shirley, 'I always assumed she was.'

It's amazing how long you can be married to someone, sleep with someone, have breakfast (usually), lunch (occasionally), tea (though rarely) and dinner (often) with someone and that still they should have the capacity to surprise you. This, I suppose, is why we marry other people and don't make do with ourselves. At any rate Victor was surprised, not so much at his sister's deviant sexuality – if Shirley was right – but that Shirley should hold a view unknown to him.

'Good God,' he said. 'That makes her a security risk!' and he could not help laughing as they crossed to say good night to his sister.

'Victor,' said Joan Lumb, 'I don't know what you're laughing about. I think there is mutiny downstairs. When I ring the bell, Acorn doesn't reply, and look, the servants haven't even begun to clear the snow!'

'Joan,' said Victor, 'surely you didn't ask them to clear the snow? It is never sensible to give orders if you know they can't possibly be carried out. Wasn't that one of Napoleon's precepts? They've all gone to bed.'

'Victor,' said his sister, with considerable petulance, 'you may know how to run a chewing-gum factory but you know nothing about servants. We are not dealing with Europeans, but with Asiatics, Hispanics and God knows what.'

'Joan,' said Victor, 'it *is* the middle of the night.'

'I wish I could ask the snow to keep sociable hours,' said Joan Lumb, 'but I can't.' (Sarcasm again!) 'I want them out there now!'

'Joan,' said Victor, 'be reasonable.'

Joan Lumb hadn't changed since she was a child. Once, in a fury because she hadn't been chosen to play Mary in the Nativity Play, she had topped the heads off every chrysanthemum in the vicar's garden, and worse, refused to say she was sorry.

'I am not a fool, Victor,' she said. 'Nor am I blind. I know there's a blizzard. All the more reason to keep the driveway clear. If we give in, the Council will too. If we do the drive, they'll be shamed into sending the snow-plough for the minor roads.'

'Joan, it's midnight,' murmured Shirley, 'and we've all had quite a bit to drink,' but no one wanted to hear that kind of thing.

'As for you, Shirley,' said her sister-in-law, 'you have not the slightest idea how to deal with servants. Do be quiet.'

'They might freeze to death out there,' said Victor. 'I hope you realise that.' He was joking.

'They can, for all I care,' said Joan. She wasn't.

'Let sleeping dogs lie,' spoke Murray, from Bella's chair by the fire, startling everyone, and all Joan Lumb thought was, 'He is foolish, he is senile, he is a poor old man, he is no use to anyone. Oh that Henry Shrapnel was alive and living at this hour!' In Joan Lumb's mind Shrapnel stayed for ever young, and vigorous.

'Talking about sleeping dogs,' said Shirley, 'do you think I should go and see how Harry has settled down?'

'I think Harry can look after himself, Shirley,' said Victor, patiently. He had quite recovered his composure. Shirley asked silly questions and he answered them. They had got along fine in this manner for fifteen years. (You may be surprised, inasmuch as Serena, Piers and Nell are so small, to discover that Shirley and Victor have been married for so long. But during the first years of her marriage to Victor, Shirley was having treatment for infertility – a condition now happily righted. I would go into the details of that, but now is neither the time nor the place.)

Victor looked forward to living the rest of his life with Shirley, and if Bella was not prepared to be a divertissement, he would continue happily enough with the ongoing melody.

'Sergei,' said Joan Lumb, 'Panza! I'm getting no reply from the servants' hall.'

But Sergei and Panza only shrugged. She had half-expected it. They were effete. They lived too much in their heads. Thought weakened their resolve. Where was Muffin? Where was Baf? Not yet returned! That did not bear thinking about, either.

'General,' she asked, 'what is to be done? I ring for the servants and they don't reply.'

'We must bow to the inevitable,' he said. 'They've gone to bed.'

He had had far too much to drink, she realised. So had everyone. It had been deliberately done. The servants had filled glasses far too rapidly.

'It's more than that,' she said. 'I feel it. Something's wrong.'

How much had she herself drunk? Gin before dinner, three kinds of wine with it, Cointreau afterwards? The lights flickered and went out. Joan Lumb spoke into the dark.

'And now the lights have gone out.'

Someone laughed. She thought it was Mew.

'No need,' said Mew, 'to state the obvious.'

Stupid, simpering girl, with her red flounces and dirty face, tottering in heels too high for her. What was she doing here anyway? She was probably in league with the servants.

'They've cut the lines,' said Joan Lumb.

'Nonsense,' said Victor, 'it's only the snow.'

'Victor,' said Shirley, 'I'm frightened!' and suddenly they all were.

25

Now by this time, as it happened, there was no need whatsoever for Upstairs to fear anything at all, at least from Downstairs (From one another was, of course, another matter.) Civilisation below stairs had been saved, or at any rate an improved status quo restored. Acorn had been deposed, and the servants slept the deep, quiet sleep of the victim whose integrity cannot be impugned, or whose morality doubted. Not for them the restless nights of the General, disturbed by the ghosts of those who would be living now, were it not that he had killed them. The snow spread its soft quiet blanket all around, and sopped up the noise of the drunken agitations up above; the telephone system between Upstairs and Downstairs was not working. Its wires had become unplugged in the struggle between civilisation and barbarity, and no one had noticed.

Tomorrow, thought the servants, drifting into sleep, packed into beds, and beneath beds, and lying filleted one onto another on the palleted floor, children entwined with children, adults lovingly with each other, tomorrow the food will be better; tomorrow perhaps justice can be won and vengeance gained: just let it not be today. All we want to do is live out our lives in peace. Miriam lies dead in the cold room, wrapped in silver foil, but she is only a woman, and all people die, and the baby is safe. Acorn lies straitjacketed and calmed by major tranquillisers on the kitchen table, where Harry's body lately lay. He is lucky to be alive. Inverness used up all his supply of clorazepate and thioridazine before he would be quiet. He is, poor man, in an advanced state of clinical paranoia. Inverness means to inform Joan Lumb in the morning: she will want to inspect for herself his rigid body, his staring eye, the convulsive movements of his hands. If he is not ranting sufficiently, Inverness will inject him with some adrenaline. He will be carted away quickly to some secure mental hospital, where he can do no more harm. If questions are asked about his legal status, Joan Lumb will have to do the answering. Poor Acorn. Do you feel sorry for him? I do. But the penalty of believing in him, following him, is death, and not just your own, but the children's. Inverness is right: boring but right. We deal in this world not in blacks and whites; blending sometimes into denim blue, just occasionally threaded through with brilliant silk. Inverness does what has to be done: he sacrifices the one for the many, and he of all the servants does not sleep well that night, but tosses and turns. Acorn's just out for the count, of course.

This is what happened.

Acorn, instead of delegating the handing round of Harry sandwiches, as he would have been wise to do, could not resist taking them up, himself, and watching the hazy, drunken crew devour them. Inverness took advantage of Acorn's absence, and addressed the servants himself.

'Friends,' he said, 'and I will not call you brothers and sisters, because we are not family. We are people of many different religions, and many different races, brought together here not by the will of Allah but by hard circumstance: trapped not by common cause but by the frailty of man and the blindness of bureaucracy. Acorn is no one's friend but his own. Lord Acorn, he wishes to be called! By what right? By the right only of his lust for power. Lord Acorn thinks he is Napoleon. Lord Acorn is insane! Agnes, are you there?'

Agnes was pushed forward by the crowd; she stood dull-eyed and slack-mouthed and wretched, quite the wrong end of the scale from the young women who fly you on Singapore Airlines.

'Acorn is mad as Agnes is mad, but in a worse way,' said Inverness. 'That is to say, from time to time both need to be shut up. He beckons you to follow him, in the same way that Agnes beckons. If you go with Agnes you catch a disease. Go with Acorn and you catch insanity itself. The madness of hate and fear is catching.'

His audience shivered. They believed him. They had felt the touch of madness.

'Acorn will lead you, in his madness, to death, pain, imprisonment, exile, and the only satisfaction you will have is the sight of blood. Acorn will have the principles, you will pay for them. Be sure Acorn won't die. No, he will take the breath out of your children's mouths, in the same way as he takes their food, and live off that.'

There was a breath of assent. Inverness was winning. But there was not much time. Soon Acorn would be back.

'Acorn speaks with a double tongue,' said Inverness. 'He talks of purity but is himself corrupt. The woman who is no woman' (he meant Mew, poor Mew: that is what happens when you wear a donkey jacket and heavy boots, the laces double-knotted, the better to ride a motorbike) 'waits for him in her bed tonight. Hilda!'

The crowd pushed Hilda forward. Matilda had gone upstairs to collect her when the trouble started. Acorn had either not bothered or forgotten all about her. She could accept her concubine status; could even cradle Miriam's baby in her arms, but she resented being forgotten. Who wouldn't?

'Hilda, isn't that so?'

But Hilda said nothing. She was afraid. Well, she was very small. Small women often live in physical fear of the men they're with: they take especial care to charm and entertain, as kittens do. That way they don't get trodden on.

'She's afraid,' said Inverness. 'It isn't love which keeps her silent, or loyalty. It's fear.'

Still Hilda kept her eyes downcast, and said nothing. Inverness decided not to continue down this particular avenue.

'Look up, Hilda,' said Inverness. 'Tell me how Miriam came to have her baby. Was that love, or fear?'

'Fear,' said Hilda, looking up. Sometimes one woman can do for another what she can't do for herself. 'It was rape.'

'Those that hath eyes to see let them see,' said Inverness, satisfied.

The crowd saw: it shuffled. Inverness promised them more meat in the pot, better heating, better lighting, a little-by-little approach to authority, proper moderate leadership – the crowd began to disperse. They understood such things would and should be accomplished on their behalf, but were bored by the detail. They were tired. It was late.

When Acorn left the drawing-room, too elated by the success of his plan to be properly careful, and pushed open the green baize door, Hastings, Raindrop and Inverness were waiting for him. A man is usually betrayed by those closest to him. Inverness tripped him, Raindrop pinioned him, Hastings bound him. In the struggle up and down the stairs, the telephone wire, which ran along the side of the skirting, became unplugged from its socket, and the old-fashioned bell-wire, rusted almost through over many decades, finally disintegrated. Inverness jabbed Acorn again and again with assorted neuroleptic drugs until he finally lost consciousness. He was strait-jacketed and stretched out on the kitchen table. Inverness dabbed some of the scum, skimmed from the surface of the still simmering pot where Harry had boiled, around Acorn's mouth, so that no one who saw him could doubt the fact that he had been foaming at the mouth.

Then they went to bed. Securing civilisation is a tiring business. They forgot to remove the pot from the flame. In Acorn's absence there was no one to keep an eye on such details. And Joan Lumb rang and rang and no one answered.

26

Remember Ivor, the chauffeur whose task it was to drive General Leo Makeshift and Bella Morthampton down to the Shrapnel Academy? On his arrival Ivor was escorted at once to a room on the third floor. It was pleasant, large, well-appointed, but lonely. He listened to the radio, but either the instrument was faulty or reception in the area was bad; he switched it off and watched television instead. A substantial supper was presently brought to him on a tray by a pretty, dusky girl – Arab, he thought – who spoke no English but had smiled and lingered as if she were offering more than food and drink. Ivor would have none of it. He opened the door for her to leave, courteously and resolutely, and closed it after her with no less determination.

He drank his pea soup, ate his gammon and chips, and some of his apple pie, and waited. Sooner or later something would happen. There was a snap, crackle and pop in the air. He could feel it. He lay on the bed to watch television, and did not take his shoes off. Debbie-Anne would never have allowed it.

When Ivor was with Debbie-Anne and the children, he wanted to be off and away. When he was off and away he wanted only to be with them. He left his room in search of a telephone; if he called his wife he might feel more settled in his mind. He wandered along deserted corridors but found no telephone. He tried doors: most were locked; or if opened, showed only interiors as bleak and functional as hotel rooms. He went downstairs, where the rooms were more luxurious, and searched there. The Shrapnel Academy, Ivor concluded, did not encourage contact with the outside world. He did not venture as far as the ground floor, where the sound of talk and laughter ebbed and flowed from behind closed doors. Someone somewhere had left a window open, or else no amount of double glazing could quite keep the wind out; scurries of cold air wafted down the corridors, carrying with them a slight celebratory smell of wine and cigarettes, and another odour besides – not so pleasant – was it meat scraps boiling or pig swill stewing? The weather outside was worsening. Perhaps he would have to dig the Rolls out of the garage in the morning? Ivor had little experience of snow. He worked mostly in the city.

Ivor went back to his room, and turned the volume of the television up to drown memories of Bella Morthampton – or were they dreams, fantasies? How was he to tell? – and at that moment the screen blanked and the lights went out.

Ivor's duty was now to be with the General. Not for nothing had he done three months' in-service training as a body-guard. A power cut can provide cover for a terrorist attack. He left his room, feeling his way along the corridor walls, coming to the open space of the stairwell, keeping to the wall, down and round, until he reached the great front hall. The door to the drawing-room was open: someone was fetching candles from the candelabras in the dining-room and Joan Lumb's voice had risen a pitch or so in its agitation. 'They have cut the lines! We are under attack! Muffin, try the telephones. Muffin, where are you?'

Ivor moved forward to be by the General's side. Joan Lumb saw him in the half dark and was alarmed.
'A stranger! Who is it?'
'Only the chauffeur,' said Bella Morthampton.

Bella Morthampton, Ivor observed, was smiling. Her teeth glinted in the light of the candle held for her convenience by Victor. Those are the teeth, Ivor thought, those are the teeth that dug into my shoulder as she clung to me and cried out. I know they are. Why did she deny me? Three times she denied me. And now I am married to Debbie-

Anne, whom I love and don't love; and whose fault is that? Why, Bella Morthampton's. The unhappy must have someone to blame.

The General moved to stand beside the great front door: Ivor moved to stand discreetly and silently at his side. 'Oh, the children, Victor!' he heard Shirley Blade say. 'Suppose they wake and are frightened!'

Muffin and Baf made their way back downstairs in the dark, so happy with each other they could not believe in bad news.
'What's happening?' Muffin asked Sergei.
'We're all drunk,' said Sergei, 'the power lines are down and Lady Lumb has finally blown her top.'

Joan Lumb, in Muffin's absence, had been to try the tele-phones herself, stumbling in the dark between office chairs and tables, barking her shin on the metal edge of the bottom drawer of one of the filing cabinets, left open by Muffin. I should have fired her years ago, thought Joan Lumb, as she lifted the receiver. She was glad to hear the blank, somehow layered, silence of the non-connected phone: she was right. The others laughed at her, dismissed her as hysterical – now they would have to change their tune.

'We haven't much time!' she cried, returning to the drawing-room, swaying from the pain in her shin. 'They're going to attack any minute. They've cut the telephone wires.'
'Joan,' said Victor, and his voice was slurred. 'Sister Joan, calm down. If the snow's brought down the power lines, why shouldn't it bring down the telephone wires too?'
'Joan feels guilty,' said Shirley, primly and aside to Victor, 'that's all it is. She overworks and underpays her servants, so she lives in the expectation of their anger. It's a form of projection. We did it as part of our "Getting to Know Yourself" course. And I didn't have to leave the children until after they were asleep, and on Monday evenings you're

hardly ever there anyway, so I didn't think I was being selfish in attending the course. Victor, can we go to bed now?'
She must have spoken louder than she intended, for she received a sudden sharp blow across the face from Joan Lumb's hand.

'Unbelievable!' cried Joan Lumb. 'This is unbelievable!' taking much the same attitude as Clausewitz, that great military tactician, when he observed the impossible actually happening; that is to say, Napoleon's Great Army in mid-flight from Moscow in 1812 – an army which went proudly out to invade Russia, 600,000 strong, returning home with 100,000 stunned, diseased and wretched men. And that, they said, was due to the snow, the weather, the unreasonable cold, that same cold which froze solid the switch of the Shrapnel Academy's emergency power supply, which should have cut in automatically when the mains supply failed. It was not, of course, the snow that killed so many. It was war. Had everyone stayed safely home in their beds the snow wouldn't have mattered in the least.

But there you are; the war was inevitable, the next step in the long march forward, initiated so long ago by Tiglath-Pileser III. Whoops, and off we go! If the right foot goes forward, so must the left. Russia had taken that step, France had to take this, to keep the balance. War kills, not weather: it kills by disease, hunger, cold, trampling, suffocation, blowing to bits, or bits off, mistaken identity, and the blunders of generals. Many, all the same, as we have already observed, prefer war to peace. Martial music, a delightful sense of togetherness, and the pride and the glory, and the achievement, and the wonder of victory and the drama of defeat, to some seems well worth the risk of death and dismemberment. Nevertheless, a good general should not spoil the fun, prick the bubble by losing 450,000 men in a forced retreat from a pointless war, as Napoleon did in 1812. But it happened, and Napoleon ceased to be the bogeyman who frightened little children, and quite lost his street credibility. Unbelievable!

'Unbelievable!' said Joan Lumb, said Clausewitz. That such things can happen in a civilised world! No food, no blankets, no shoes for the troops, limbs lying everywhere, no telephone for Joan Lumb and the Wellington Lecture in danger. Clausewitz went home and wrote *On War* – the bible of generations of military men throughout the world. Shirley turned to Victor, weeping and saying, 'Your sister hit me. Why did she do that, Victor?' and Joan Lumb demanded that a party be sent down to investigate the servants' intransigence. The General agreed that this should be done, as much to allay Joan Lumb's fears as anything; the males of the party formed themselves into a double file, three deep – Ivor with Baf went first, as the youngest and strongest, then the General and Victor, then Sergei and Panza, who were thinkers rather than doers. Intellectuals, that is to say. Murray was nowhere to be found, and no one cared. Least of all Bella.

Ivor put his shoulders to the green baize door, and pushed. It did not budge. Baf tried, and then the others, and then all together. It was stuck firm, and the more they pushed, the harder it seemed to stick, which was not surprising, since the door opened inwards. But you know how it is – once you have decided something is lost – like the bottle opener – there's no finding it, although it is under your nose. Once you have decided something won't work – like the steam iron – there is no extracting steam from it. The brain, expecting disaster, fails to find the obvious solution. No one thought to pull the door: all pushed.

Joan Lumb did not seem so foolish now. The men looked at each other.
'Hmm,' said the General. 'Locked out! Snowed in! In the dark! With no communications. It doesn't look too good, does it, Baf?'
'Perhaps I should bring the knife box down,' said Baf, 'just to be on the safe side.'
'Don't even think of it, boy,' said the General.
The eyes of both men sparkled in the candlelight. The

General looked younger and Baf older, which was what each wanted. Some people thrive on emergencies. The men still clustered around the green baize door: the women edged nearer.

'Knife box, what knife box?' demanded Joan Lumb.

'*The* knife box,' said Mew. 'The secret weapon?' It was half a joke, but she shouldn't have made it. Joan Lumb heard.

Victor said, 'We're taking this too seriously. The door may simply be jammed,' but his voice lacked conviction, and he convinced no one. He would have fired himself, had he so spoken at the Board Room table. But it was late, he was tired, he had been more upset by Bella than he knew, and the temperature was dropping every minute. The boiler ran on oil but was sparked by electricity. Shirley ran upstairs with a candle to be with the children.

At that moment Murray came back from the Gentlemen's Rest Room, where he had been retching up the sandwiches. 'Dog,' he said. 'What I ate was dog. There was dog meat in the sandwiches. Only dog meat does this to me. There's no mistaking it.'

And that was the end of the peace; the beginning of the war.

27

A lasting peace! How we all want it, or think we do! Napoleon was the first one to talk about it, invading Russia in its name, and many is the war since that has been waged on its account, and many the government persuaded to part with enormous sums of money, thinking that perhaps this will be the last time, this'll show them, this will keep them in their place! Only of course it never does. Peace may look good to governments but is only the quiet time an army needs to recover from the last war and prepare for the next. It can't be expected to last, and perhaps it shouldn't. Peace is good for agriculture, but bad for the economy, bad for love, and bad for civilian morale. Civil unrest, blasphemy, discontent and crime flourish in times of peace. No matter! Napoleon got all the way to Moscow, saying peace when he meant war, with the Russian army retreating before him. Sometimes they couldn't retreat quickly enough, and the armies met up and pride demanded a battle, or an incident, as the politicians had already learned to call it. Sixty thousand Russians died in one particular incident-packed sixty-mile stretch of retreat. Clausewitz described these as 'trifling losses'. (A matter of comparison. No one ever managed to count the Russian army, it was so very numerous.)

A quick description of the Battle of Borodino, on the way to Moscow? You can bear it? The ins and outs of it have been fascinating owners of lead soldiers and the players of computer war games ever since. Does that tempt you? This sector against that: this wildly shifting line of artillery, that scramble up this slope, this thundering cavalry, that roar of mighty cannon? The Russians lost 58,000 men, more than one in two. The French lost a further 50,000 from their remaining 130,000. The cannons, we know, fired 120,000 times (someone had been counting) and corpses of every European nationality lay so close together it was impossible to walk without treading upon them. Ditches were overflowing with the torn bodies of horses and men. The chief surgeon of the Grand Army performed 700 amputations, and 74 per cent were successful. Not bad! And the Russian wounded, they said, didn't let out a single groan. The French were much criticised for screaming and moaning when wounded. When darkness came these wounded and dying were abandoned. But still, but still, let us remember with Joan Lumb that the manner of living is more important than the manner of dying.

Napoleon moved on to Moscow. He chivalrously waited at the gates for the Russian army and its refugee entourage to move out of Moscow before making his triumphal entry into the city. The times, you see, were changing. PR was important. The world must witness triumph, not carnage: and such few citizens as were left in Moscow obligingly turned out to cheer. People will always cheer soldiers, no matter what side they're on. It was unfortunate that much of the city burned down once Napoleon was installed in the Kremlin. The Russians blamed the French for the fire. The French maintained it was Russian arson. The argument as to whose was the responsibility of the burning of Moscow continues to this day.

Napoleon waited for an emissary from Alexander to acknowledge his victory. But no one came. What was he to do? There he was, camped with his 80,000 remaining men, all exhausted, the end of a wedge driven 120 miles into Russia, in a hostile, burning, starving city: the troops unharvested, winter coming – how was this war to be brought to an end? Wars must end, do end, always had ended – people parley, give in, acknowledge they were wrong. One side submits: the other goes home, victorious. Pieces of paper are signed: trumpets sound, peace reasserts itself, hands are shaken, courtesy visits exchanged. But the Russians just weren't playing by the book.

162

And the snow got nearer. The Grand Army, which was composed of Germans, Poles and Italians as well as the French, were a long way from home. They were hungry and dirty and bored: they stopped being an army and turned into a nasty rabble, and Napoleon noticed it. He tried writing to Alexander, but Alexander, safe in St Petersburg, wouldn't even answer the letters.

Alexander did issue a proclamation. 'Let no one despair. Indeed, how can we lose courage when all classes of the realm are proving their courage and constancy?' Despair, courage, constancy. They fly like a flock of noisy birds, these abstract terms, these appeals to the unreal, over smoking ruins, over legless men, over howling women and blasted children, over the clawed hands of the burned; they drop their shit, and are gone.

The Great Army pulled itself together, picked up all the available loot left in Moscow – silver, gold, coins, ornaments, jewellery, icons, whores – and set off relieved and singing back towards Smolensk. 'Your hunger will finish at Smolensk,' Napoleon told his troops. The man was an idiot. How could it? He had passed through the place before. Every last chicken had long ago had its neck wrung. Such crops as had survived in the rancid fields had rotted. How do the dead and dying achieve a harvest home? The bureaucrats who went ahead of the army sold everything and anything edible that was left and made off with the money. Oh, glorious Napoleon, great conqueror, crazed with self-esteem! Did you think Nature would slow its pace, people change their natures, for your convenience?

As the Grand Army retreated, the Russian army now advanced. What a Pas de Deux that was! The Russians at least had food. They brought it with them from the South. Armies go less hungry than peasants. The French were, simply, starving. They ate their horses. Then they ate each other. The road to Smolensk was scattered with emaciated bodies and the limbs were gnawed away, observers said, and not by rats. The French dragged hostage prisoners with them: few survived, they were shot, bayoneted, or clubbed if they staggered or lagged behind. Russian serfs, men, women and children, were recruited to ambush, harry, hack down and exterminate the French. (They did this with alacrity, thus worrying their masters somewhat. You shouldn't let a tiger get the taste of human blood. They were right to worry, as it turned out. Look what happened next!) The French army had long ago abandoned its loot, its baggage, its guns, its sick, its wounded. And who had the energy left for a whore? They passed through Borodino, scene of the great battle. The plain was covered with the rotting remains of horses and stiffened men half-eaten by wolves; it was littered with broken weapons, and rusty sabres. Oh magnificent Battle of Borodino!

It was mid-November before the limping Grand Army reached Smolensk, and of course found no food. They took the hungry, icy road back to Paris. But now the snow had begun. At one point 7,800 infantrymen and 450 cavalry, together with 8,000 dispossessed non-combatants – old men, women, children, who thought they were safer with an army, any army, than anywhere else – all under General Ney, were surrounded by the Cossacks and asked to surrender.
'What, me?' asked Marshal Ney. 'Surrender? Never!' and chose to escape over the iced-over Neiper river. Brave Ney stepped first onto the ice (it cracked but held). On, on, he cried. And those behind cried forward and those in front cried back! And over they went! Ney made it to the other side, and so did 800 of the troops. But some 7,000 souls fell through the ice and died; and the 8,000 helpless – the sick, the wounded, the women and the babies – were left on the wrong side of the Neiper, to be slaughtered by the Cossacks. Which they were. Oh, brave General Ney, who wouldn't surrender!
One more river to cross. The Berezina, this time.
'Unbelievable,' said Clausewitz once again, when his boss, General Wittgenstein of Prussia, attacked what was left of

Napoleon's army on the snowy banks of that particular river. Ten thousand died there. Another classic battle, much played and replayed by enthusiasts. The battle plan? I could give you a map but I won't. You'll find accounts of it in any library, much thumbed.

While the Battle of Berezina waged, the Great Army engineers tried to keep the bridges open for the retreat. But they were jammed up by thousands of undignified and undisciplined non-combatants pushing, struggling, screaming for a foothold, tearing, panicking. The Cossacks approached, hacking as was their fashion from their vantage point of horseback height. This one's head, that one's arm – and meanwhile, as cannon fire shredded men by the dozen, the bridges collapsed. Hundreds were trampled underfoot and suffocated in the blood-stained slime.

'Unbelievable,' wrote Clausewitz, but why he should have found it so I really don't know. War was his trade, his pride. Or did he just like the troops to die more cleanly, with grace and style, and the non-combatants not getting in the way? 'Defence,' wrote Clausewitz, 'is the strongest form of combat.' Attack the best form of defence. Well yes, sometimes. Sometimes not. The sheer swing of the words gives the Clausewitzian phrase the force of gospel. Clausewitz is to the military as the Bible is to Christians and *Das Kapital* is to Marxists. Marx sat in the British Museum and projected a future from the past, as was the fashion at the time, and these writings, these uneven gropings towards understanding, became the law of nations, because they were so admirably, if lengthily, expounded. Writers can't resist the heady swing of language: ceaselessly they subordinate truth to a good phrase. 'All happy families resemble each other –' Tolstoy. Pschew! Nonsense! Clausewitz looks over a campaign or so and says, 'War is a continuation of policy by other means.' And neo-Clausewitzians take it as gospel and a million missiles spring and the whole world cowers. 'Unbelievable,' says Clausewitz, when he looks at actual war, at the remnants of Napoleon's Great Army. Oh, the intoxication of words, the vulnerability of flesh at the word's mercy!

'What ghastly scenes have I witnessed here,' he wrote home to his wife, after Berezina. 'If my feelings had not been hardened, it would have sent me mad ... I saw only a small fraction of the famous retreat, but in this fraction all the horrors of the movement were accumulated. A man crawled to the broken bridges, the red stumps of his legs leaving two red trails in the snow: a woman who had fallen half through the ice had frozen there, one of her arms half-severed, the other clutching a breathing, suckling baby.' Reader, I *know* it isn't easy. But if I can write it, you can read it. It is important to consider the detail of these things from time to time, and still take seriously Joan Lumb's premise that the manner of living is more important than the manner of dying. The man with the stumps may well have had a glorious war until that moment. Who are we soft liberals, readers and writers, to deny it to him? If Clausewitz himself, while experiencing horror at the carnage, did not turn his back on it, but went on to enjoy it, and make a system out of it, and manage it, so shall we. Destruction is liberating to the spirit, both of the destroyer and the destroyed, and there's the nub of it. Turn over the stone of disgust and a little bright, shining, mystical insect crawls away. It is the soul. If there is no reality left, no houses, no bridges, no bags of flour; if all the people are mashed into pulpy shreds only then can there be the pure energy of being left, the soul, and that soul is heroic –

Would you like a verse from Homer's *Iliad*, in the Richmond Lattimore translation? Joan Lumb hasn't read it: she doesn't read poetry. But most of the young students who attend the Shrapnel Academy have been brought up to admire it, and understand very well what Homer says.

'So, friend, you die also. Why all this clamour about it? Patroklus also is dead, who was better by far than you are. Do you not see what a man I am, how huge, how splendid and born of a great father, and the mother who bore me immortal? Yet even I have also my death and my strong destiny, and there shall be a dawn or an afternoon or a noontime when some man in the fighting will take the life from me, also, either with a spearcast or an arrow flown from the bowstring.' So he spoke, and in the other the knees and the inward heart went slack. He let go of the spear and sat back, spreading wide with both hands; but Achilles drawing his sharp sword struck him beside the neck at the collar-bone, and the double-edged sword plunged full length inside. He dropped to the ground face downward, and lay at length, and the black blood flowed, and the ground was soaked with it.

But I don't suppose the dead young woman with the severed arm and the still living suckling baby had read the *Iliad* or could take much comfort from Homer. I wonder if the baby lived? Unlikely, with the temperature as low as it was. But you never know. Perhaps Clausewitz himself took pity on it, and waded through the icy torrent to rescue it, and it was a little girl, and she grew up to be a Mills & Boon heroine? Oh, you never know. And the mother's misfortune the baby's good fortune? Such things happen.

Napoleon managed to get 80,000 people over the river: but 40,000 of these perished in the next stretch of road, from cold. Frostbite removed hands, feet, noses, ears. Skin turned purple, then blue-brown, then black, as it rotted from living bodies. Fingers and toes snapped like dead twigs. No food was so rotten or disgusting as not to find someone to relish it. No fallen horse remained uneaten: no dog, no cat, no carrion, nor indeed the corpses of those that died of cold or hunger. Men even gnawed at their own famished bodies. Some went insane. Some just lapsed into lethargy, known as the Moscow Depression.

The Russians, pursuing, suffered as much as the French. The temperature fell to 40° below zero. Napoleon tried to turn and rally his men, but a further 12,000 had perished by then, and what good were those who were left? Gunmen with their hands frozen off! Infantrymen with no feet! Weapons are a great deal more reliable than people: the lesson was learned. Progress, progress! More and better weapons, of a non-labour-intensive kind, that's what's needed in modern warfare, that's what we've got today, not human flesh with its propensity to rot and disintegrate. It took six miserable men to fire a single Gaundeval 12-pounder cannon, with its lethality index of 940. And only six brave but (at that time) happy men to drop one 120 KT bomb over Hiroshima, with its lethality index of 4,908,600. Mind you, these latter six were well-educated and highly trained, and their aircraft kept warm for them.

Okay?

Now it is time to get on with the story, to turn our attention back to the startled group in the hall of the Shrapnel Academy, that shrine to the memory of Henry Shrapnel, who invented the exploding cannonball in 1804. The temperature is dropping slowly but perceptibly. The great basket of logs, chopped and split by Hastings, is all but empty. Joan Lumb wishes she had not been so extravagant with both wood and coal in her early attempts to drive out the unwelcome cooking smells which had plagued the evening, and the reason for which had now become apparent.

'Dog!' Victor exclaimed, when Murray appeared pale and trembly from the bathroom. 'You mean we've eaten poor Harry in the *sandwiches*?'
'It can't have been our Trish or Trixie,' said Muffin, thankfully, 'because they're away at the kennels.'
Muffin had prevailed upon Joan Lumb to have the two house dogs sent away for the Wellington Weekend. They were liver spaniels. Although perfectly accustomed to

trousers and well-polished shoes, they became over-excited by pale high heels, fine stockings, beige silk shirts and gold bangles, and could, and often did, muddy and score the fronts of the lady guests in the enthusiasm of their welcome. Joan Lumb had resented the necessity of shutting the animals away, while yet recognising it existed.

'Perhaps they're not in the kennels at all,' said Joan Lumb, her courage quite restored by this attack on dumb animals. 'Perhaps they were in the caribou patty – oh, I could throttle them all with my own hands!'

And so she would, had the servants been rash enough to get their necks in the way. To balance the death, even the possible death, of Joan Lumb's dogs, at least a dozen men and women would have to die. This is an attitude common to those who feel they have a divine right to power. Only put them in a situation where they can exercise it and they will. My inconvenience, your major misfortune! Caligula of Rome avenging the death of his horse, Heydych of Holland, getting even for his burst tyre, caused the deaths of thousands. Beware of anyone saying 'I'd like to wring their necks.' *They would if they could.*

The General took command, Joan Lumb having been disqualified by those signs of distress and hysteria which earlier had underlined her female state – it is no use being proved right after the event. You have to seem to be right all the time, if you are not to lose credibility – and Victor having disqualified himself by virtue of his decision at the age of twenty-three to go into business, and not the army. Baf was too wild and too young for command, and Sergei and Panza had no gift for leadership, nor claimed to have. Murray was currently too ill to be considered, although his expertise would no doubt come in useful. They were most grateful to have him amongst them. Ivor was a servant. These matters they settled swiftly and easily amongst themselves, some things being said, others thankfully left unsaid. Mew prepared a speech which went 'But this is sexism. I can see that Joan Lumb is a token man, but you haven't even

mentioned Muffin, Shirley, Bella or me,' but prudently she
didn't deliver it.

Baf wished to make a battering ram out of a settee in the
hall and break down the green baize door, but the General
would have none of it. A posse of armed servants might well
be waiting on the other side of the door for just such an
event. Although those at the top of the stairs would of course
have the advantage of height, those below outnumbered
those above to an unknown factor—

—at which Joan Lumb interjected, 'We have thirty-six
servants on our pay-roll. Though I think on occasion they
do have their friends to stay. But I'm a generous employer.
I don't fuss too much about detail—'

—to which Muffin replied, 'Joan, if you ask me, there are
three thousand down there—'

—and Joan Lumb said, 'I didn't ask you.'

—anyway, an unknown factor, and although there was no
evidence of arms—

—at which Victor interjected, 'They have the kitchen
knives. If they can kill Harry and make us eat him, they
can do anything—'

—no evidence of arms, as the General repeated, but lack of
evidence was no guarantee they didn't have them. So the
storming of Downstairs was out—

Baf contented himself with aiming a few hefty blows and
leaping kicks at the green baize door. Panza pointed out
that the servants might erupt up the stairs at any moment
with heaven knows what weapons, or what intent. So a
party was organised to move a heavy bureau bookcase,
which contained a complete set of *Samuel's Military History,
1860–1900*, impenetrable volumes if ever there were such

things, in front of the door which divided Upstairs from Downstairs. Another party – the egress group – was sent to confirm what already most knew, that snow to the depth of between four and six feet now made all exterior doors unopenable, and that escape from the Shrapnel Academy was impracticable. A further group went up to bring down Shirley and the children, and check that all other rooms in the Shrapnel Academy were empty – all were – and no bands of aggressors hiding in the upstairs territory – none were. Shirley wept a little, and said, 'If they are capable of leaving innocent children alone and unprotected, they are capable of anything.'

The egress group came back to report that the only access to Downstairs was via a single laundry chute in the extension wing, on the south-west corner of the building. They had listened, but all was quiet. Yes, a person could wriggle up – or down – with difficulty. Ivor was sent to man the chute, and report back at once any signs of activity.

The General then called a Council of War. The Council – which included the female members of the group – sat around that same table where lately they had celebrated the rather indigestible rewards of peace. The ceiling of the dining-room was low, and offered the illusion that it was a little less cold here than anywhere else. They sat in the same order as they had at the Eve-of-Wellington dinner. Joan Lumb thought there was something missing, and presently realised what it was. It was her adoration of Murray, which had been, she now realised, an almost tangible presence at the meal. Now it was as if the spirit of Jesus had abruptly vanished from the Last Supper. She felt bereft, and shivered, not just from cold, but foreseeing that the spirit of love would not touch her again in this world. Her courage had failed: she had turned it away. She had had her chance, and blown it.
Blankets and quilts were brought down from above and the Council wrapped themselves in these. A few nuts and raisins

were discovered in cupboards, and the General generously had his bottle of Laphroaig brought down. But all remarked on how the sealing of the green baize door had reversed the normal order of things – now Downstairs had everything – at least in the way of food, drink and warmth – and Upstairs had nothing!

But Joan Lumb said, 'Hardly nothing! *We* have brains, expertise, training, discipline, organisation. *We* are a crack corps, *they* are an undisciplined rabble!'

Mew had another speech prepared, to the effect that perhaps Murray was in error in believing that the sandwiches were filled with dog meat, that the non-response of the servants to the bell and telephone was coincidental, as was the lack of heat and light, that the green baize door had merely jammed, and that they should all just go to bed and see what things looked like in the morning. But she didn't deliver it. She didn't like the way Joan Lumb kept looking at her, and occasionally muttered to the General, behind her hand, rather rudely. Mew had been brought up not to whisper in public. Her mother had been only patchily insane: in the good patches she was an excellent mother.

Joan Lumb said, 'Did you say something, Miss—er—'

Mew replied, 'No. Except I suppose it *was* dog meat.'

Murray retched again; Muffin, with Baf as escort, went to fetch him some Kaolin and Morphine from her bathroom cupboard. They returned promptly – the exigencies of the situation, alas, ensuring it – and when they did Baf was carrying his knife box. Eyes turned towards it: those who knew what it contained, and those who didn't.

It was late, but no one was tired. Adrenalin trickled out its silver threads of energy and excitement. They had been taken by surprise, when the lights went out. Even Joan Lumb had lost her nerve. Never again! Now their task was to puzzle out, somehow, what was in the enemy mind.

'We must have information,' said Baf, 'because information is power.'

'To predict their actions,' Murray said, 'we must understand their motives.' The Kaolin and Morphine was making him feel worse, not better.

'We must know their numbers,' said Panza, 'because that will inform their actions.'

Each statement seemed as convincing as the last. If only words were weapons, how strong they would be!

Bella sniffed. 'What a horrid smell,' she said. And indeed there was. Trails of black, stinking smoke were beginning to drift under the dining-room door. The party took candles, and traced the smoke back to its source, in the drawing-room. Even in the dim light it could be seen that gusts of the disgusting stuff were billowing back down the now almost cold chimney, and swirling like fog into the room. They were under attack! They were to be choked to death! Suffocated! The women withdrew at once to the foot of the stairs.

Murray seized a rosewood occasional table, snapped it into pieces and flung it on the embers to restore the fire. The room was evacuated, and the door slammed shut. Joan Lumb ripped one of the best tapestries from the dining-room wall and stuffed it into the gap between door and floor. Muffin was sent to the library to fetch sticky tape – only she knew where it was – and the door was taped firmly around. Fortunately, the door was well made, and a good fit. No trails of escaping gas could be seen: the attack had failed. They were safe!

In fact the smoke had stopped flowing from its source. What had happened was that the stockpot had finally boiled dry, and Harry's bones had been charring nastily. There is nothing horrider than the acrid, oily smell of burning bones. No wonder the fumes were construed as enemy action! If you had smelt them, you would think the same. The stench had woken Matilda, who had gone to the kitchen to see what was happening. She had moved the pot, and plunged it under cold water – holding her nose – and gone back to bed, not without a quick, nasty pinch of Acorn's smooth young cheek as she passed. Strait-jacketed and unconscious on the kitchen table, he could do her no harm.

28

The supposed gas attack on Upstairs happened at 2.17 on the Saturday morning. By 3.15 Mew had been stripped naked, had escaped torture and rape by the skin of her teeth, and had been tumbled down the laundry chute to join her 'friends'. A ferocious discharge of CS gas from Baf's miniaturised cylinder went after her.

This is the timetable of what happened:

2.20   Mew goes upstairs to change out of her heels and flounces and back into donkey jacket, jeans and boots. She is feeling distinctly unsafe and the atmosphere downstairs is not good.

2.30   Baf recognises Mew as person who refused lift.

2.35   Joan Lumb accuses Mew of being an enemy agent. She refused Baf's lift because she had a rendezvous with the servants. She had posed as a journalist from *The Times*; then changed her story when she thought she might be rumbled. Had anyone there read the *Woman's Times*? No? Obviously, it did not exist. She had spent time the wrong side of the Green Baize Door.

2.50   Muffin attests that Acorn had been in Mew's room, and that Mew had been taking photographs, including one of Baf's knife box.

2.55   Mew is stripped and body-searched   a task delegated to Sergei and Panza, and threatened with rape and torture if she does not reveal the whereabouts of the camera. She has been trying to tell them for some time. Only when Victor appears, tut-tutting, do Sergei and Panza seem able to hear.

3.00   Camera discovered and destroyed. Shirley, weeping, intercedes with Council for Mew's life, and succeeds. 'We are not barbarians. We leave that to the enemy.' Which of them said that? Could have been any of them.

3.05   Mew is frogmarched to the top of the laundry chute and tumbled down.
        'What are you doing?' asks Ivor, horrified. He has been dozing at his post and escaped war fever. He sees Baf open the knife box, take out the cylinder and, with the General's approval and that of the entire Council, direct it down the laundry chute after Mew. 'Keep back,' says Baf to Ivor. 'This stuff is really heavy.' Ivor dives down the chute to save Mew if he can. Baf hesitates. But the General nods, and Baf discharges the cylinder and all retire back to the dining-room to consider their next move.
        'He is obviously one of them,' says the General to Shirley, who is most upset. 'Now you must toughen up, my dear. This is war.'

Bella really seems to be enjoying herself. How bright her eyes are, and she has her lipstick with her, so that her mouth becomes darker and more garish hour by hour, and her white skin is almost translucent in the candlelight.

Sometimes weapons work. Sometimes they don't. Sometimes they go off with less power than expected; sometimes a great deal more. Baf's cylinder of CS gas misfired. He was, after all, a salesman, not a technician. He succeeded only in aiming the device, not in actually firing it, but who was to know that? Mew and Ivor ended up a good deal safer in the servants' quarters than either of them had been Upstairs, Mew tainted as she was by feminism, and Ivor by his membership of the servant classes.

The episode at Fort York in 1813 was one of those memorable ones, when there's a far bigger bang than anyone expects.

Fort York today stands on what must be one of the most expensive pieces of real estate in Canada. It is an open flat, grassed square, in the centre of Toronto. It has agreeable Georgian proportions, and is surrounded by a wooden palisade. Here tourists, visitors to the city, and school parties go to discover what the past was like and how their antecedents lived. They can taste turkey pie and flummery in the cook-house, served by wenches in low-cut dresses, look over the officers' living quarters, admire the still ticking grandfather clocks, and have demonstrated to them just how this and that worked by lolloping, healthy, tall young Canadians dressed in the uniform of the York Queen Rangers or of the 16 US Infantry, it seems now to make little difference. The War of Independence is all long ago, and quite who was fighting whom, and why, is best forgotten by adult and child alike. For are we not all now at peace? This place, pleasant enough in sunlight, becomes quite grim and haunted when the sun goes behind a cloud. It is a phenomenon observable at the sites of other spectacular disasters: Juhu Beach, outside Bombay, where the first 707 crashed: the sports stadium at Brussels; the Firth of Forth, where the Tay Bridge collapsed – places don't seem to recover; it is the human race which just goes blithely on.

Now what happened at Fort York was this. The American army, under the command of Brigadier Zebudon Montgomery Pike, invaded the Fort. They sailed across the harbour towards the fort clearing, in a formidable force. The British commander eventually ordered the retreat: the garrison was to be abandoned: the men were to blow up the arsenal. A fuse was set, lighted, the men withdrew, the expected explosion happened. The York magazine went up. But they had underestimated what was in there. The whole ground shook for miles around; a cloud rose, in a most majestic manner, assuming the shape of a vast balloon. It was the nearest thing to a nuclear explosion the world had seen before Big Boy in New Mexico in 1945. Timber, stones, debris, rained down from the sky upon British and American alike. Pike was killed, so were 368 of his men, and 222 were injured, many later to die. A party of forty British regulars was killed outright. Both sides sat down together and wept. This was not what they had meant at all. Officers fell in the same way as soldiers: it was not war, it was disaster. It was not planned, it was an accident. But all that's another story.

It was now time for the Council of War to look at the situation in the light of the timeless verities of combat. Joan Lumb thought this showed cold feet, a retreat from action into theory; and shivered and sulked a little when they took no notice. The snow had begun again: it beat with such ferocity against the window panes the glass seemed to tremble and there was a kind of disagreeable, inexorable beat in the wind, a thud, thud, thud. Was it quickening, building to some kind of climax? She couldn't bear it. She wanted to cry, but how could she? She, Joan Lumb.

These were the headings the General and his team worked to:

No. *1*   *Offensive action is essential to positive combat results.*
Exactly! Pumping CS gas down the laundry chute had been exactly that. Now the strategy had to be followed through. The plan was to pierce the Green Baize Door, and lob Baf's grenades down, thus destroying the enemy outright.

No. *2*   *Defensive strength is greater than offensive strength.*
True: and Downstairs are certainly superior in numbers. But not in weapons! The servants still lived in the Age of Muscle: thanks to the Knife Box, Upstairs is in the Age of Technology. (Doubts as to the morality of Baf's Knife Box had simply evaporated. It was as if they had never been.)

No. *3*   *Defensive posture is necessary when successful offence is impossible.*
Should the offence fail for any reason, fall-back positions would be on the stairs. The Academy

178

would be defended floor by floor, to the death, if necessary.

No. 4 *Flank or rear attack is more likely to succeed than frontal attack.*
Since the gas attack had been down the laundry chute, and that would be seen by the enemy as frontal, the next attack should be down the stairs. That was what the Council had in mind.

No. 5 *Initiative permits application of preponderant combat power.*
One gas attack had equalled another, but now the Council wrested the initiative out of the hands of the enemy.

No. 6 *Defenders' chance of success is directly proportional to fortification strength.*
An unknown factor, this. The Council rather regretted having disposed of Mew. Further interrogation might have yielded necessary information. However, what was done was done.

No. 7 *An attacker willing to pay the price can always penetrate the strongest defences.*
Nothing is for nothing. There might well be a price to pay. That price might even be death. There was no doubt that the pumping of the CS gas, the flushing out of the vermin, would be construed by Downstairs as an escalation of the conflict, and retaliation must be expected, of the undisciplined, individual kind. The General hoped the Council were aware of this. They were. And prepared to pay the price! Baf revealed that the new form of CS gas used in the cylinders could cause death to women and children in some circumstances: that is to say, anyone below a certain body weight. More harmful, on the whole, to foreign nationals than Western Europeans, in whom, of course, it could cause wasting, paralysis, and other side effects . . .

No. 8 *Successful defence requires depth and reserves.*
Should the gas attack have for any reason failed,
should the servants retaliate before offensive action
could be accomplished, and come welling up the
stairs like a host of cockroaches, Baf's weapons
would be waiting to challenge them, wipe them
out. Baf was to set them up, in readiness.
'Look here,' said Baf, 'that's something of a risk.
I'm a salesman, not a technician.'
The General said the risk was acceptable.
Weaponry should not be kept idle in reserve
position.
Napoleon's two greatest defeats – at Leipzig and
Waterloo – were the result of this failure to give
proper credence to Verity No. 8. Baf was to get
going. The bureau bookcase was moved aside. The
grenade rocket on its silver matchbox was
positioned outside the green baize door, to mow
down possible attackers surging up the staircase.
The tiny, tiny machine-gun was placed at the
Council's fall-back position on the first landing, for
use in the unlikely event of the first defensive bar-
rage failing. It looked just like a child's toy, left
idly on the stairs. Piers stirred in his sleep on the
dining-room sofa. He had just such a toy at
home.
'Interesting to see if it works,' said the General.
'Quite,' said Baf.

No. 9 *Superior strength always wins.*
It was possible, the General said, that agitators
and subversives had provided the servants with
weaponry, but he had not had that impression
from Mew. The Council would win! Defeat was
unthinkable.

No. 10 *Surprise substantially enhances combat power.*
'Let's not hang about,' said Victor. 'Let's just go
in and get 'em! I have a meeting on Monday

morning. When Gloabal send the helicopter, I don't want any unnecessary delays.'

But the General continued, relentlessly, with his checklist.

No. 11   *Firepower kills, disrupts, suppresses and causes dispersion.*
The advantage of a grenade attack through the door would be that the dispersion of the enemy forces would then be no problem. They'd all be dead. So powerful were the grenades, Baf claimed, although only the size of a cherry each – the Knife Box carried six in all – that what explosive power did not destroy, shock would. Burial would be an eventual problem, and the prevention of disease, and so forth, but these problems could be deferred until later Council meetings.

No. 12   *Combat activities are often slower, less productive and less efficient than anticipated.*
The overkill factor of the grenades was great enough for Upstairs not to worry too much about lack of efficiency. These were, in fact, ideal field conditions in which to test the weapons.

No. 13   *Combat is too complex to be described in a single, simple aphorism.*
'I think we've got it licked this time,' said the General. 'I think for once the single, simple aphorism will be ours. "We wiped 'em out!"'

The thirteen verities having been checked and discussed, there was no way of avoiding action.

While Panza, Sergei, Victor and Murray removed the bureau bookcase from its protective position in front of the Green Baize Door, Baf took out his knife box and prepared the grenade attachment. The six grenades were to follow one another down the launcher, a thin, sleek, shiny tube. Baf set the notch for maximum effectiveness. Set lower down the scale – according to the PR handout – the weapon could be used merely to deafen and stun, and so was invaluable for the control of certain crowds. But this was war! Should the enemy come rushing up the stairs, should any survive the onslaught of Baf's grenades, they would encounter the machine-gun or bullet sprayer, which, when armed and directed, issued a spray of tiny pressurised bullets which grew larger and larger as they flew through the liberty and lightness of air. These would penetrate and explode, so great was the force behind them, when they struck solid matter or flesh and blood. If any survived this, they would then have to face the righteous anger of their attackers, which all believed would be invincible.

Baf chipped away at the green baize door with an ordinary penknife. It took him a full half hour to make a hole big enough for the insertion of his firing tube

The General looked at the six cherry-sized metal balls and wished to God he had a proper, solid, old-fashioned machine-gun: a tilt of Baf's hand and he was as likely to get his own forces as the enemy's but it couldn't be helped. The proper way to use the grenade launcher was to embed it in the wall – unnoticeable to the casual eye – and activate it electronically from a distance, but needs must, and there was an emergency manual activator, and this Baf must use. Still, he would be interested to see what happened. If the weapons were as effective as Baf suggested, he might well make representations to the Ministry of Defence, on their behalf.

'Ready,' said Baf. He looked around the faces which crowded around him. Their future, their safety, was in his hands. He was frightened: an emotion he had never felt in his life before – too young for the responsibility of life and death. Supposing it went wrong? 'Go in there and get 'em!' said Joan Lumb.
'Blast them to hell!' said Victor, her true brother in the end. Breeding will out.

'Baf, darling, do what you must,' cried Muffin. 'I'm with you all the way.'

'Get 'em quick,' said Murray, roused from his nauseous stupor, 'before they get us!'

And there were other, more pompous, remarks from Sergei and Panza: 'Their foul and aggressive deeds must not go unpunished. This riff-raff must be taught a lesson—'

'But supposing there are children?' ventured Shirley. Victor was finally irritated with his wife. She was hopelessly domestic.

'If there are children,' said Joan Lumb briskly, 'they are not there legally, and the sooner they aren't there the better.'

And Bella spoke at last, 'Children? So what? They would only grow up to be criminals and murderers, like their parents. Fire, Baf! What's the matter? Chicken?'

So Baf overcame his hesitation – pure superstition – and let the cherries fall into the dark on the other side of the green baize, and pushed the button in what he thought was the correct way – one, two, three, four, five, six times – and on the sixth press that was the end of everything, so suddenly no one had time to say or think anything at all. Baf was, after all – and he was the first to admit it – a salesman and not a technician. The armed, but not fired, CS gas cylinder was activated by the grenade blast and sparked an explosion in the napalm thrower and the tiny howitzer and the strategic nuclear cannon and in the space of seconds that was that. Baf had neglected to close the knife box, as when a child he had once neglected to put the lid back on the carton of fireworks on November 5th. Trouble was bound to ensue.

29

Only two people survived the explosion the night the Shrapnel Academy went up. The other 331, for there were 333 souls in residence that night, all died. The ones who escaped were Mew and Ivor. They owed their good fortune to the fact that the small half-underground section of the Shrapnel Academy which housed the laundry chute remained relatively intact. It was a later Victorian addition to the building, and faced on the outside with Portland stone, which largely protected those inside from the blast and heat. The blast was enormous: snow was melted across a one-mile diameter. Bricks, mortar, stone, furniture, bodies, statues, trees, snow, all hurled into the air, and whirled and whizzed about a bit, and fell again, in shreds.

Edna the taxi driver saw the explosion from the cosy room twelve miles away where she nursed her cold and sat out the blizzard. She saw a singeing, blinding glare on the other side of the woods, so that the line of distant hills could be seen quite clearly, as she sometimes could on one of those cloudy, damp evenings when visibility was oddly greater than ever it was on the brightest day.
'That's really beautiful,' she said aloud.
Then there was a surprisingly short sharp bang, and then other noises, messier and more protracted, whooshings and roarings and gnashings, and then a sudden rush of wind which rattled her windows, and then silence. The snow had stopped: she could see stars above: it was as if the explosion had whipped the clouds away: only over where the Shrapnel Academy was – well, had been, thought Edna, because that was surely the Shrapnel Academy going up, and now what would happen to her taxi trade? – a dusty cloud obscured the sky.

The two survivors stayed where they were and waited for help to arrive. They knew it would. Heroic efforts would be made, in spite of the snow. Police, ambulances and fire engines would presently arrive. Insurance investigators and journalists would drop from the sky. Cameras would whirr, newsreader voices lower in respect for so many dead. Such a terrible tragedy! Funds would be raised, every possible kindness shown. The good will of man would be made apparent. Mew would have a story for the *Woman's Times* so extraordinary it would not be believed, and not printed. Angered, she would accept an offer from *The Times*, which paid a good deal better, and did not discourage the wearing of high heels. Ivor would go home to Debbie-Anne and stop brooding about Bella Morthampton: there is no point in lusting after the dead.

Reader, I know you do not like this ending to the story. It seems a cheat just to blow everything and everyone up. I wish there was some other possible ending, but there isn't. That's the way the world ends, not with a whimper but a bang, the way it began.

But I will give you something else – just a soupçon, as my grandmother, always a finicky eater, would say when accepting soup. Grass and flowers have grown up through the rubble of what used to be the Shrapnel Academy. It takes only a season or so for Nature to reassert itself. An owl swoops to take a mouse: a spider shrouds a fly. Snap, snaffle, nibble, crunch, gone! That's Nature for you. But little eddies of lively air do tend to form at a certain point, at first-floor level, above the rubbly green. You can even see the motes dancing on a bright evening at just about the place where Mother Teresa was situated, there where Baf and Muffin took their spectacular pleasure, and butterflies dancing where the cupboard beneath the stairs used to be, which Acorn and Hilda would frequent. And if you listen you seem to hear a voice, mixed up with the songs of birds. It is Joan Lumb: she is speaking to Murray. She is saying, 'Murray, that was not what we meant at all: it got out of

185

control. But, Murray, wasn't it *all* fun!' Ah, fun: oh, Henry Shrapnel! And how forgiving the God of Love is, after all, that he should have given Joan Lumb another chance to love Murray and suffer for it, for certainly not in this life or the next will Murray ever love Joan Lumb.